LUKE CHRISTODOULOU

THE
CHURCH
MURDERS

VINCI
BOOKS

Vinci Books

vinci-books.com

Published by Vinci Books Ltd in 2026

1

The publisher and the author have made every effort to obtain permissions for any third party material used in this book and to comply with copyright law. Any queries in this respect should be brought to the attention of the publisher and any omissions will be corrected in future editions.

A CIP catalogue record for this book is available from the British Library.

Paperback ISBN: 9781036713591

The EU GPSR authorised representative is Logos Europe, 9 rue Nicolas Poussion, 17000 La Rochelle, France contact@logoseurope.eu

By Luke Christodoulou

Greek Island Mysteries

The Olympus Killer
The Church Murders
Death of a Bride
Murder on Display
Hotel Murder
Twelve Months of Murder

To my daughter Ioli.
You crazy, little bundle of joy... I love you.
Also, a huge thank you to my editing and proofreading team!

¹ And I saw when the Lamb opened one of the seals, and I heard, as it were the noise of thunder, one of the four beasts saying, Come and see.

² And I saw, and behold a white horse: and he that sat on him had a bow; and a crown was given unto him: and he went forth conquering, and to conquer.

³ And when he had opened the second seal, I heard the second beast say, Come and see.

⁴ And there went out another horse that was red: and power was given to him that sat thereon to take peace from the earth, and that they should kill one another: and there was given unto him a great sword.

⁵ And when he had opened the third seal, I heard the third beast say, Come and see. And I beheld, and lo a black horse; and he that sat on him had a pair of balances in his hand.

⁶ And I heard a voice in the midst of the four beasts say, A measure of wheat for a penny, and three measures of barley for a penny; and see thou hurt not the oil and the wine.

⁷ And when he had opened the fourth seal, I heard the voice of the fourth beast say, Come and see.

⁸ And I looked, and behold a pale horse: and his name that sat on him was Death, and Hell followed with him. And power was given unto them over the fourth part of the earth, to kill with sword, and with hunger, and with death, and with the beasts of the earth.

—Book Of Revelations: Chapter 6, 1-8

(King James Bible)

Chapter One

The winter sun vanished behind the verdant hills that bordered the outskirts of the Megalopolis of Athens and light surrendered its place to darkness.

The same dilemma every December. Did I hate that it got dark from 5 pm more than I hated the suffocating heat of the summer? Spring; now there is a perfect season. Maybe I was just getting grumpier as I unwillingly approached the threshold of my life's fifth decade.

I turned on my Audi's headlights and smiled upon hearing the sound of the skies rumbling above. I loved driving in the rain and my black car needed to shed off gathered dust.

Route 56 is a bore. One long straight line of a road, always loaded with traffic and with a view of endless grey dull apartment blocks. Others would have taken the Metro to Piraeus, but I never did have much so-called *common* sense. I was in no rush to see the department's shrink and my empty apartment did not mind if I returned home early or late. I turned off the motorway and headed down to Akti

Miaouli. Outside, the wind was busy playing around with dried up leaves and the clouds above shot down fat drops of rain.

I parked opposite the modern glass building that housed Dr. Ariadne Metaxa's private office. She worked office hours, every Tuesday and Thursday, at police headquarters, but I preferred to attend her private practice. It gave me time to unwind from work and put on my fake, friendly and joyful mask before visiting her. I did not need a psychologist meddling inside my brain.

I needed her clearance to get back to active duty.

I exited my car and stood for a moment in the pouring rain, enjoying every drop that ran down my face before running across the bustling road. Everyone without an umbrella was running to cover themselves from the menacing drops. Some get cleansed by the rain, some just get wet. I pushed the buzzer-bell that bore her name and waited for her assistant's annoying voice to be heard. I do not mean to be harsh, but if you are going to hire someone to answer the phone and the door, at least avoid a girl with such a grating voice.

'Doctor Ariadne Metaxa's office. How may I be of assistance?'

Lower your voice.

'Captain Papacosta. I have an appointment.'

'Come right up, Captain. The doctor is waiting for you.'

Of course she is. I have an appointment.

I pushed open the heavy metal door and walked towards the elevator. Dr. Ariadne's office was located on the 14th floor. An entire side of her office was made of glass, offering an incredible view of the busy port of Piraeus; one of the few perks of visiting her here. That and the much more comfortable chair.

Her lanky assistant was already standing and had her hand, palm up, indicating the office's wooden door.

'Go right in, Captain,' her words came out from behind crooked teeth, accompanied by a warm inviting smile. Good hearts can always make up for shrill voices and bad dental hygiene.

'Thank you,' I exhaled the words and smiled back as warmly as I could. As I walked into the dimly lit room, the door closed behind me. Dr. Ariadne rose from behind her huge mahogany desk where she had been preoccupied reading a medical journal. She walked towards me slowly with an air of confidence that lived with her permanently; her red hair stroking her bare shoulders and her emerald eyes glowing as they focused on my pitiful appearance. I stood there with soaked brown hair, drops of rain combined with mild sweat running down my face, wearing a plain old pair of jeans and a white T-shirt under my black leather jacket. In contrast, from her cleavage to her knees, a red, tight dress draped Dr. Ariadne's body, silver high heels graced her feet and she looked as if she had just walked out of the hairdressers. She wore red well. Like fire, it shined upon her white pale complexion. She must be one of the whitest women in Greece. She surely avoided the Greek wrinkle-inducing sun. A highly intelligent woman, just a step away from forty, with a Mensa membership to prove it.

Her soft hand fitted into mine.

'Good evening, Captain. Lovely rainy day, is it not?' her modulated voice filled the artful and minimally decorated room. She sat down first in her crimson armchair and her flat-line smile invited me to sit in the armchair facing hers. Below us, ships were entering and exiting the port, enjoying a good wash courtesy of the plummeting water. I twisted and I turned until I found a comfortable position to relax in. I knew I would be here for a good hour, but I asked anyway.

'Doc, you know why I'm here. I need you to give me the all-clear to get back into the field. It's been a week and I cannot take another day sitting behind a desk doing the chief's paperwork!'

'I could sign the paper and you could be on your way, back to your work in under a minute. However, that would mean I was not doing my job. You were sent here for a reason.'

'I don't need another psych evaluation,' I snapped. Dr. Ariadne was my evaluator when I arrived in Greece two years ago and asked to join the police force here. With my background as a homicide detective in New York, a murdered daughter and being a lonely unsociable divorcee, it came as no surprise being sent to the good, old head doctor. Eight sessions on and Dr. Ariadne deemed me fit for duty.

'This is not an evaluation Costa, and you know it. It is just typical procedure when a Police Captain throws his computer out his office window,' her reassuring, smooth, sweet voice flowed through the space between us and calmed me down. 'You saw tens of dead bodies all at once. It is okay that you were upset,' she continued, maintaining the same tone.

'I was upset for not solving the case!'

'Do you always solve the case, Captain?'

'No. This is real life. Not a movie or a book where an ending is needed.'

'Do you feel that this case needs an ending? Do you need closure?'

'The case is closed. That's closure... I just wished I had figured it all out sooner. Perhaps I could have saved them.'

'Don't beat yourself up. I understand it is a pyrrhic win for you, but keep in mind, you save lives every day in your line of duty. Just a few months ago, you made headlines by bringing the Olympus Killer to justice. You saved your partner's life and protected many others.'

I smiled slightly at the thought of my partner, Ioli. I had not seen her since she returned to Crete. She received three months leave with daily physiotherapy recommended. After Christmas she would be back in action. She was being transferred to Athens where we would be officially teamed up by the chief. Homicide division for the Greek Isles.

'Ioli was cleared by her shrink,' I hinted.

Dr. Ariadne exhaled deeply. She stared straight into my brown eyes for a good minute. 'Let's make a deal. I clear you today and whenever you need to be cleared again, and you agree to cut the tough guy act and come visit me once every fifteen days.'

I started to form an argument in my mind, however, one single word came out that surprised us both.

'Done.'

Chapter Two

A month ago

Salamis Island is one of the closest islands to Athens; two kilometers away from the main port of Piraeus. That is everything I could tell you about the place before November 21st came to existence. It was a typical morning, with me holding in my beer belly as I drank my third morning coffee, surrounded by mesomorphic, Herculean-build police officers down at the department. I nodded my head as they complained about the ongoing economic crisis and how they barely made ends meet.

One phone call changed the dull day.

'Captain? You are requested on line three. Possible murder case on the Island of Salamis,' police officer Andrea Loukaki informed. I swallowed my coffee in one quick, sloppy sip and headed towards the phone located somewhere on my junk-yard of a desk.

'Captain Costa Papacosta.'

'Good morning, Captain. This is Police Sergeant Jason

6

Galanos. A body, male, was reported found in a trench near Batsi beach forty minutes ago. I am at the scene now. The body seems to have been stabbed several times and from what I can tell, has been out here quite a while. I cannot get closer as the body is too far down. I have contacted local rescue workers to assist...'

'I'm on my way. I'll be picking up the coroner too. Secure the crime scene. Photograph everything, touch nothing.'

I walked out of the station's back door and exited into the vast parking lot. Excitement fueled my pace and before I could dial the coroner's number, I was standing beside my car. The steering wheel was hot, the air stale and unpleasant to breathe. I looked up and squinted at the unusual sizzling November sun. *Enough with the heat already.*

'Jacob Petsa,' the coroner's voice came through my cell phone's crackling speaker and interrupted my fearful thoughts of another rain-free year in Greece. Jacob sounded out of breath and was obviously chewing down food of some sort.

'It's nine o'clock in the morning. What the hell are you eating in the morgue?'

'Costa! Malaka, what you up to? And to answer your question; breakfast, of course. There is an amazing bistro just round the corner that makes an exquisite full English breakfast. And guess what? With coffee, only five Euro! You see, ever since the kids left home, Maria has been trying to put us on one diet or the other. Oats are not breakfast, my friend, that's for sure! I once told Maria that I was not a freaking rabbit and I demanded a man's meal. You should have seen her face, she... Costa? You there?'

'Yep.'

'You normally interrupt me by now,' the jovial coroner said and chuckled.

'I was going to, but then I needed to satisfy my curiosity. I always wanted to know if you would ever stop!'

'Well, now you know! What've you got?'

'A dead male in Salamina. I'll be outside the morgue in five minutes.'

There was no reply. Jacob did not even bother to end the call. He placed the phone on his cold stainless steel surgery table and hobbled towards his breakfast. No crispy bacon was going to waste, not for *any-body*.

Chapter Three

Batsi beach is considered one of the top beaches of the shrimp-shaped island. Not that it meant much. Salamis was not a tourist island; it gathered more locals during the summer than foreigners. Now, just a step away from winter, it looked abandoned. I looked around at the few scattered village houses, standing on the hill slope nearby and rejected the idea of finding a witness. I ordered two men of the local police from the main city, Salamina, to go door-to-door nevertheless. It struck me as weird that someone would dump a body so close to the coast. I mean, either bury him where you killed him or throw him in the water as you came this close. A body in a ditch is a panic drop-off. My thoughts were all over the place. I closed my eyes as we approached the crime scene and exhaled. *Focus, Costa, focus.*

'Good morning, Captain. This way.' Jason Galanos was a rather short Greek. He was a brawny bull-necked type of guy with distinct Greek coloring and a distinct Greek nose. He moved few facial muscles as he spoke and behaved in a formal and respectful manner; something unusual nowadays in the police force, especially by those under thirty. I followed the speedy officer up the dirt path, with my eyes exploring the surrounding environment. Dried up country-side with pale green bushes and stubborn olive trees growing out of the rocky grounds. Dr. Jacob Petsa huffed and puffed as he walked behind us, complaining about nearly everything.

'Maybe Maria's idea of a diet is not as bad as you think...' I dared to tease with my good old friend.

'Maybe I'll push you down the ditch and leave with two bodies!' he declared and laughed out loud. His laughter echoed along the hillside and the rescue workers ahead turned to see who was so happy on approaching a murder scene. The serious-looking Sergeant had placed four iron bars around the ditch and created a rectangle with the classic yellow police tape.

The workers had already prepared the much-needed hooks and ropes for our descent to the body. I am sure I saw a worker double-check the ropes as he saw my height and Jacob's width. I looked down into the wide trench. The body lay ten meters below, face down. He wore only a pair of ripped bloody boxer shorts.

'Who found the body?'

'A young couple from Thessaloniki here on holiday,' Jason was quick to answer. He pulled out his little black detective notepad and continued 'Andreas and Eleni Karambetti. Aged twenty-eight, both of them. Here for the extreme sports. There were paragliding from the hilltop when Eleni started screaming and pointing down. I have their statements and they are staying in a guest room nearby if you wish to speak to them.'

'Great work Jason,' I said, admiring the youth's way of presenting himself. Old-fashioned and controlled.

'Let's go pay our victim a visit,' I gave the OK to the men in charge to tie us up. 'Lower down the spotlights too.'

'I'm getting too old for this shit!' Jacob declared as they gradually lowered us into the earth's cavity. We landed a few feet away from the body and untied ourselves according to the instructions we received from above. I steadied the two spotlights and switched them on. Bright white light spread throughout the ditch. I left one where it landed and carried the other to the opposite side of the poor man. Our shadows played a macabre puppet show on the hard surface of the trench walls. I photographed the body's back and zoomed in on his wounds. Violent, messy entry wounds all over the place. Hands pushed by hatred executed this crime. Worms and flies were continuing their feast on the flesh and tiny, nibble bites indicated that mice and other small rodents occupied and roamed the trench at night. Around the body was dark blood spatter. No clothes or other items were to be seen. Jacob knelt beside the body, fixed his glasses upon his nose and squinted his eyes as he wore his off-white latex gloves. They don't give out medical examiner awards, but if they did, Jacob would have a whole trophy cabinet. I stood aside, giving him his five minutes.

'Let's turn him around,' the simple order came and I assisted in slowly turning the body to face us. We both gasped in shock at the sight of the stabbed face. The eyes sockets were severely cut, both eyeballs and several teeth were pushed in and parts of the neck were missing, having been stabbed several times. The victim's chest was stabbed so many times that there were entry wounds upon entry wounds, forming bloody star shaped stabs. Even his upper leg had stab marks. Wounds were of all depths and widths. This was either the work of a maniac who, blinded by the moment, struck frantically or as my inner gut feeling screamed out, the work of multiple murderers.

'Shall I start my monologue?' Jacob sought to see if the voices in my head were ready to quieten down and listen.

'Shoot away.'

'Male. Early thirties. Time of death? Three days ago. Might be less, but definitely not longer. The body's temperature is the same as the environment, the greenish-blue color has spread to most of the skin and the gases in the body tissue are starting to form blisters. He has been stabbed dozens of times, there is no way of knowing which was the original blow, however, all the injuries occurred in a matter of minutes; indicated by the blood coloring and clotting around the wounds. All other bone and tissue damage was most likely caused by the fall that happened post-mortem.'

I straightened the victim's head and snapped away. We would need to identify the body. The sooner, the better.

Chapter Four

The local police station -if it can be called that- reminded me of a studio apartment. All in the one room, excluding the bathroom. On the left, Jason's cheaply bought office with an outdated, dusty and rusty computer, a Greek flag, an icon of Saint Nicholas, a picture of his proud parents and an Olympiacos coffee mug that served as a pen and pencil holder. On the right, file cabinets, a holding room, separated by bars, that looked unused and the yellowy bathroom door. Batsi, population 212, was the most populous of the dozen villages Jason was in charge of. He lived a quiet life during the winter and was responsible for maintaining the peace when visitors flocked to the beaches in the summer. This was most likely his first murder case.

'May I?' I asked as I pointed to his office chair.

'By all means,' he rushed to answer and quickly turned on his computer.

'Coffee, Captain? I make a great, strong, Greek coffee. And I have freshly made loukoumia. My aunt makes them.'

'Sounds divine. Make it sweet,' I replied and with the

word sweet, thought of Jacob Petsa on his way back to Athens with the body. He surely would have loved a coffee and a couple of Greek Delights before the autopsy.

It took my ageing eyes a minute or so to connect the wire into the camera and then the other end into the USB port. This was Ioli's part. I wish she was here, but I knew her body and heart needed and deserved a rest after last summer's drama.

I successfully uploaded the photos to the computer's desktop and managed to email them on my third try to the homicide department in Athens. I requested they searched thoroughly through missing persons files; someone must be looking for him, he had been gone for over three days. If not through our database, then on 'Light in the Tunnel', a successful missing persons TV program. No mention was to be made that he was dead. A sketch was to be made from the photograph and appear with the caption 'Family looking for missing son. Last seen in Salamina.'

'Here you go, sir,' Jason said, placing my coffee and a little white plate with four cubic loukoumia by my side. He sat down on a chair in corner of the room and remained there, drinking his coffee. I could not decide if he was unsociable or just the type of guy that did not talk much. I preferred to believe the latter. I drank my coffee in silence and ate all four sweets. Before devouring the fourth, I asked 'No loukoumia for you?'

'I avoid such sweet temptations. Doctor's orders,' he replied with a rascally smile, possibly reminiscing the days when he would eat a whole plate of these heavenly goods.

'I should be getting back. Hopefully, the coroner will be finished with the autopsy by night and my people will have an identity for me. If any interrogations need to take place on the island or if I request any further assistance, I will be in touch.'

He stood up at once and extended his right hand. He had a firm grip and opened the door for me to exit. *They sure don't make them like this anymore.*

Hours later, I was sinking into my once white leather desk chair. My back reminded me of the two hours it had taken me, in heavy traffic, to get here after I drove off the car ferry that connected Salamis with the mainland. All of Petrou Ralli Street was filled from top to tail with cars, cargo-filled trucks and people-filled buses. I slowly moved through the scenery of monstrous grey apartment blocks with a billion antennas sticking out the top, reaching up into the rainless, orange colored clouds.

I stretched my arms up high, closed my eyes and found serenity in picturing the pork chop I was planning on ordering later that night. I inhaled without a sound through my nose and exhaled with a light sigh from the mouth. No luck with the victim's identity. I hoped that for once the TV would be helpful and give us a lead.

Chapter Five

The next morning came and found me sunk into the same chair and -my worst pastime- on the phone.

First call was to Dr. Jacob Petsa who confirmed the date of death and that all injuries came from the same blade. He supported my theory of multiple attackers as a few stabs were made by a left-handed person and varied in intensity and depth. The victim was healthy and had eaten fruit and cheese as his last supper.

After the coroner, I called Sergeant Jason Galanos, who with complaint painting his voice, announced that no witnesses had been found and they had not had any luck with the victim's identification. No one in the nearby villages had ever seen our blond-haired victim.

As the handset found its nest, my right eye caught a glimpse of Sergeant Demetriou hovering behind me.

'Captain, there is a woman down in reception. She saw the victim's sketch on TV and wishes to speak to whoever is in charge.'

'Set her up in interrogation room three,' I ordered,

thinking how weird I was to prefer a certain room. It was exactly the same as the other interrogation rooms, but I always used three.

'Right away, sir,' her words came out with speed from her full Angelina Jolie-ish lips and off she went to fulfil her goal, her ponytail swinging from side to side. After relieving myself in the gents and splashing some cold water on my face, I walked into my favorite interrogation room.

A red-haired woman approaching sixty, with hazelnut eyes and worry all over her face, sat uncomfortably in the hard cold police chair. She was fully dressed in black -the sign of a widow here in Greece. She held her cup of coffee tightly and took anxious quick sips. She looked up at me and gave her best attempt at a smile.

'I am Captain Papacosta,' I introduced myself as I sat down opposite the distraught woman.

She is his mother!

'I understand you have some information concerning the man in the sketch you saw last night?'

'Funny thing for a family to be locking for their son and not provide a name. Is... my son... hurt?' she struggled to form the question.

'I am sorry to inform you that yesterday we recovered your son's body from the island of Salamis.' In all my years delivering bad news, I have come to realize that there is no reason to beat around the olive tree. It only prolongs the agony.

Her hands shook as she held her face. The realization that her baby boy was no longer a part of the world of the living clouded her face. She maintained all her courage in an effort for answers.

'How?' she asked with trembling lips that were being watered by silent tears.

'He was murdered...'

A chilling scream that turned into uncontrollable sobbing caused me to pause and let her grieve. I spoke no words of comfort. I know too well that words mean nothing at a time like this. Your soul gets shattered and neither time nor words can put the pieces back together. You just find a way to keep on breathing. No pain can be compared to that caused by the death of your child. You will never love anyone or anything as much as your child.

'Who would want to murder Alex?' her hollow stare reflected the hole growing inside her heart.

'That is what I want to find out. And I need your strength and focus to do so. Alex you say? Surname?'

'Alex Panayiotou. I am his mother, Voula. He was my only child...'

'Did he live with you?'

'No, no... Alex was too independent to accept being pampered by me. I live in my village, Avlona. Alex continued living in the apartment he stayed in as a student, here in Athens. He loved the big city. The noise, the theatres, the girls.'

'Did he live alone? Have a girlfriend? Did he work somewhere?' *Slow down, Costa. Don't get carried away. Let her tell her story.*

'He... worked at The News of Athens. He was a reporter. Last time he phoned home, he said he had broken up with that beautiful little thing he brought home for Christmas. Eirini was her name. I liked her. She was good for him...' She stopped, lost in her thoughts.

'When was the last time you saw him?'

'I am not a bad mother.'

'No one said you were, Mrs. Panayiotou.'

'I saw him last...around Easter. He seemed well and

happy. I called him every Sunday and he would listen to my mindless chit-chat about the village and all my old lady's gossip. He was a good boy, my Alex. That is why it shocked me when he stopped answering my calls.'

'When did this start?'

'Around July. And then, one day in August he finally picked up and he shouted at me. He never raised his voice, not even as a wild teenager.'

'What did he say?'

'He said I was annoying him and I should finally cut the umbilical cord, and that I should stop calling him... He hung up on me and ever since his phone has been switched off. I worried, but with my hip and the farm, I could not come down to Athens. So I called Eirini.' She paused and I could sense something was bothering her. She hesitated.

'Mrs. Panayiotou, anything you say, is between you and the police...'

'I don't want to blacken his memory.'

'What was Alex...'

'Drugs,' she delivered the word wrapped up with despise and hatred. 'Eirini said he got messed up with drugs and that he quit his job and kicked her out of his house. My boy would not do drugs, I raised my voice at her and hung up. It is hard for a parent to accept such a thing. You bear children, you shower them with sense and morals and let them fly away and you hope that all you taught them does not slide like rain off an umbrella.'

'I will pay his boss a visit and may I have the phone number for Eirini?'

'Of course. Find out who killed my boy Captain,' she said with a steady voice and stood up. 'Now, may I see him?'

'I will arrange for a police car to take you to the hospital. I must warn you, Mrs. Panayiotou, he was stabbed to death and he suffered injuries to the face. Prepare yourself...'

'I guessed that much from the sketch. I thought, why not a photograph?' She swallowed hard and wiped her tears. 'I will survive, Captain. Now, all I seek is justice.'

Chapter Six

The News of Athens is widely known as the capital's most prestigious and bestselling newspaper. The 'bad tongues' as we say here in Greece, would gossip that sales soared because the tabloid offered music CDs, nature DVDs and an array of lifestyle magazines free with every sale. Its main offices were housed in the Athens Tower, a glass wedding cake type skyscraper, occupying the first eight floors. I entered the vast, front lobby flushed from my fast-paced walk, and approached the oval-shaped reception booth. A dark-haired girl with wires coming out of her ears, lifted a 'one minute, please' finger at me as she continued to talk into the microphone that originated from her ear.

'Good morning, how may I help you, sir?'

'I need to see the editorial chief, Mr. Aggelou?'

'Do you have an appointment, sir?'

'No, I am...'

'It will be impossible for him to see you today. If it is urgent, I could schedule you in by...'

'Now,' I said, flashing my badge. 'Just direct me to his office and inform him the police is coming up. Thank you.'

I exhaled as I entered with the rest of the sardines into the glass cage that lifted us up to the eighth floor.

I followed the receptionist's directions and found myself up against yet another receptionist/secretary. She quickly rose to her feet, informed by the desk below, to welcome me.

'Good day, sir. Mr. Aggelou is expecting you. May we offer you a cup of coffee?'

'No, thank you.' I pushed open the door and entered the most spacious office I had ever stepped foot in. The painted light blue walls were decorated either with fine art or framed front pages. A modern wooden bar counter occupied the corner on my right, while on my left was a 70" TV, split into cells that showed the various major news channels of Greece. In front of me was Mr. Aggelou's colossal desk. Expensive wood -no doubt- with the latest state-of-the-art laptop and tablet by his side. I walked over and shook his extended hand. The view behind him was breathtaking. All of Athens unfolded all the way up to Lycabytus Hill.

What kind of person puts the view behind them? The sunsets must be majestic to watch from here.

'Have a seat... Mr?'

'Captain Costa Papacosta.' I situated myself opposite him in a strange-looking black and white armchair. Sitting down, I realized that the chair's patterns were different photographs from around the world.

'And to what do I owe this visit?' he asked with apathy. A man used to knowing everything and whose every guest took up less than two minutes of his precious time.

'Alex Panayiotou.'

'What did that firecracker get himself into, this time?' he smiled with admiration and a quiet chuckle.

'He was murdered three days ago.'

The corners of his smile took the road downwards, his broad shoulders fell and his blue eyes seemed to turn a pale shade of grey. He opened the top draw on his right and lifted out a thick cigar. He mumbled a 'Do you mind?' to which I shook my head that I did not. He lit it and smoke spread out into the room. As he blew out the dense smoke, it danced its way over to my nostrils. I breathed in the polluted air, took it down to my lungs and reinforced my opinion that smokers never really quit.

'Can I offer you a cigar, Captain?'

Oh, yes, please do. 'No, thank you. I quit years ago.' *And have smoked at least thirty cigarettes since then...*

'Murdered? By whom?'

'That is what I am trying to figure out. I realize he used to work here. When did he quit exactly?'

'Quit? Alex never quit! He never quit anything in his life. Stubborn little one he was. One of my rising stars!'

'His mother had a different impression. So, when was the last time you saw him? When was he last at work?'

'Last July.'

'That's four months ago.' I tilted my head slightly to the side and assumed my pose of inquiry.

Did he quit or not?

Mr. Aggelou leaned forward and started to narrate the events of their last encounter.

'12th of July it was, I am sure of that. I was up to my neck with coverage of the British's Prime-Minister's visit and Alex came barging in with that hot-shot look all over his face. He was sweating with excitement as he declared that he had the story of a lifetime. If I had a penny every time I heard *that* line! He was certain that a monastery in Salamina had... a document.'

He paused.

'A document?'

'Captain, I do not know if he was right or wrong. However, in the case that he was right, I must request that anything said here between us, stays between us. Especially now. If he's dead, he might just have been right. That crazy boy who I thought crazier, could well have been right. Well, I'll be damned...' he said and turned to face the crucifix hung on the wall, up high. His three fingers met and he *did his cross* as we say here in Greece.

'What did Alex believe he had found?'

'He did not reveal his sources, but he was dead certain... poor choice of words... he was certain that the monks were hiding an Evaggelio written by Jesus Christ himself.'

'He sounded sure of this? A Gospel by Jesus himself? I am not a deeply religious man, but I imagine if something like this were true it would be...'

'The story of the century! I had my doubts, but I built myself up based on hunches and I really liked the kid so I gave him 3000 Euro and six months to deliver the story. He walked out of my office with a wide grin and a fire in his soul. I haven't heard from him since.'

'Did he reveal how he might go about getting the story?'

'No...'

'Would he go undercover as a monk?'

'I guess so. Those isolated monks tend to keep to themselves. They would never do something as blasphemous as to talk to a journalist!'

'Do you think Alex would have spoken to anyone else besides yourself? Maybe team up with another reporter or a photographer?' *He certainly did not tell his mother or girlfriend. He lied about getting fired, probably lied about the drugs too, to isolate himself or perhaps to be accepted as a monk. Most monks leave their earthly life -as they call it- behind, most because of a haunting past such as drug abuse. It would have been a great cover for him to infiltrate the monastery.*

'No, no... Alex was a tiger. He hunted alone. And a story this big, he wouldn't have told his own mother! Damn, he wouldn't have told me if he did not need the budget and the time off work!' He laughed and his large belly wobbled under his blue shirt. 'Get me his killer, Captain and I will owe you,' he said, pressing his index finger on the wooden surface of his desk. 'The media can be really kind if it wants to be.'

'I will do my best. Thank you,' I said and stood up. Politics were never for me. I had no plans to be in charge of a department or become chief. I'm barely in charge of myself most of the time. We shook hands and I was on my way. All the way back to my office and straight to my computer. Monasteries in Salamina. Search. Three. One in Salamina, town center, dedicated to the Virgin Mary. Saint Lawrence Monastery in a small coastal village on the other side of the island from where the body was found and Saint Nicholas Monastery, isolated on Mount Maurovouni, thirty minutes away from the crime scene. Only St. Nick's did not accept pilgrims or any sort of visitors. In a matter of minutes, I was on my way to cross the narrow strait and meet up with Sergeant Jason. We were going to pay the monks a visit. After I ate, that is. *Never interrogate on an empty stomach,* Ioli advised me once. She was right. An empty stomach only caused a bad temper and made it difficult for the brain cells to concentrate solely on the case. She would not have approved of the oily pita bread with my fatty pork gyro that sat on my passenger's chair next to my deep-fried fries, as I drove onto the ferry boat. My guilt was pushed away by the first bite and the sensation of chopped up meat melting in my mouth.

You haven't eaten gyro if you haven't eaten it in Greece.

Chapter Seven

Death had always been a friend of his. Since childhood, death had excited him. The way the eyes went hollow, the decay of the skin, even the putrid smell was a high. The whole dying and rotting away process as the soul burned through the body and ascended to the sky to be judged.

He carefully locked the old wooden door behind him and descended awfully narrow mud-made steps. The candle's light was flickering from the air below. Air was running to escape and meet the free air howling outside through the pitch black night. He paused for a moment as he reached the basement below. Two doors on his left, two on his right; two empty, two not. He decided upon the fat one. More skin should make his task easier. He unlocked the rusty door and struggled to push it open. Sobbing began before he could light the cell's candles.

The fat man's eyes rushed from side to side in a frantic attempt to see who had entered the room. The only thing he could see was the crucifix on the moldy wall opposite him. He had lost sense of time. It had been two or three days since he was captured; he remembered being gagged and blindfolded, he remembered his clothes being ripped off his body and being watered down by a high pressure hose. Then, everything went blank. He awoke tied face down on a freezing cold, steel table. His whole body was aching, but the thirst was worse. Through his raggedy gag, he begged for water, he begged for mercy; the shadowy figure did not react, did not ever enter his vision. The room reeked from his bodily releases. He felt ashamed lying there in his own dirt, exposed, scared.

This time the shadowy figure came close.

Yes, death excited him, but he would not kill the *fat guy* tonight. No, he had work to do first. Tomorrow. Yes, tomorrow he would burn. He walked over to the small cabinet in the corner, opened it and took out a bottle with some sort of see-through liquid. He emptied the fluid all over the obese man's back. An action that made him squeal like the pig he was.

'Stay still, pig! The more you move, the more this is going to hurt!' he whispered into piggy's left ear.

He dug into his pocket and pulled out his well-sharpened barber's razor. With a smile that spread like wildfire from ear to ear, he lifted the bloody blade from its wooden home. He looked down upon his human canvas and stroked it with the sharp tip of his blade. In the darkest corners of his mind, he pictured the design and pushed the blade into the skin. He cut half an inch deep and started to draw. He had to be careful. Not too deep. His Piggy had to be alive for tomorrow.

Chapter Eight

I hoped my air freshener and the air blowing in through my car's opened windows would kill the smell of my kebab before I reached the poor excuse of a police station. Sergeant Galanos was standing outside waiting for me. His dark brown hair glued down, his shirt's top button sealed, his clothes ironed to perfection, his black boots reflecting the afternoon sun.

'Sir,' he nodded and sat in the passenger's seat. Not one for words, this one.

'Good day Jason. I guess you know the way or shall I plug in my GPS?'

'Keep going straight. At the T-junction, turn right, then first right all the way up and from then on, Maurovouni mountain will always be in sight.'

He spoke more mechanically than my GPS girlfriend.

'First murder case?'

'Yes,' he admitted and went silent, lost in his thoughts. I filled in the silence and chatted away about my first case and a bunch of clichés of how you get used to it.

The monastery was truly a marvel of Byzantine architecture. It occupied the entire mountain's peak and its outer stone-brick walls continued down the mountain's steep sides and became one with the lone pinnacle. Similar to a Venetian castle of the Dark Ages, there was just the one entrance, sealed off by a gargantuan, tongue-shaped, wooden gate. In full contrast, an electronic doorbell with a moving camera were built in, next to the gate. I parked to the side, amongst vexatious weeds and wild roses. I stepped out of my Audi and gazed towards the horizon. Greece made it so easy to fall in love with the ocean. That is when I realized that I had stepped on a colony of ants, probably killing half the population with my heavy black army boots. I also noticed that Jason was standing by the bell waiting for me to give him the OK to ring it.

'Let's see who's home,' I raised my eyebrows and said.

The bell echoed in the silent, open space.

'Hello?' a scratchy unfriendly voice came through the speaker.

'Hellenic Police, open up.' Jason's manly voice grew even deeper.

'Do you have any women with you?'

'No, we are two male officers...' I said and was cut off by the automatic opening of the gate.

The inner courtyard was vast and filled with fruit trees and multiple vegetable patches. From behind the trees, rose the majestic stone-built church, dedicated to Saint Nicholas. It had two bell towers, one on each side, and in the middle a huge dome outgrew them and was home to a large, marble Tesseract crucifix. Oval, stained glass windows circulated the well-preserved building, and through the open door, the golden iconostasis was visible. On both sides of the church, a row of ageing arcs led to the monks' cells.

'Stay here,' the order came from the hooded monk that appeared out of nowhere. 'The ygoumeno will be with you shortly,' he continued, avoiding eye contact, and walked away through the labyrinth of tomatoes and lettuces. I strolled around, satisfying my curiosity while Jason stood statue still. He coughed as he saw the monastery's abbot approaching, to attain my attention. I was busy fiddling with the mud which filled the gaps between the stones that formed the wall. I was amazed that grass and mud could keep the large rocks together.

The abbot was a medium height man in his seventies, with crow's feet around his eyes and a deep scar on his left cheek that journeyed all the way up and became one with his forehead wrinkles. He was underweight, same as most monks, due to strict fasting and lack of meat. His head had long since said its goodbyes to most of its hair and the silver lines originating from the side and stretched to cover the top were fooling no one.

'Welcome to our monastery, gentlemen,' he spoke in a whispery manner that forced you to stretch your ears and wish you could turn up the volume on the old man. His hands were steadily interlocked with each other, mostly covered by his two sizes bigger brown monk overalls, and he bowed slightly as he welcomed us. 'To what do we owe this visit?'

'I am Captain Papacosta and this is Sergeant Galanos. We are investigating a murder case. The murder of this man, Alex Panayiotou,' I said and flashed the photograph of the youth beneath the abbot's thin almond eyes. He moved no facial muscle, but the pupils of his eyes moved around his green irises, similar to annoying flies hovering above your Sunday roast.

'I am abbot Serafim,' he, in turn, introduced himself

with a cold smile. 'No, I have not seen this man before. Was he a pilgrim here? I do not meet them all and even if I did, at my age, my memory is not what it was.'

'No, not a pilgrim. I believe he came here to be a monk.'

'When?'

'Three months ago...'

'Impossible. We haven't had a new monk in our order for over two years now.'

'Is there anyone else I could ask? As you said, your memory is not all what it used to be.'

His eyebrows came down a few degrees and his smile turned into a line.

'You believe I am lying to you, Captain?'

'Lying is such a harsh word. I know how these orders work. You are a brotherhood and brothers protect each other. You take in many with questionable pasts. I think that if Alex showed up here, trying to get away from his drug addiction, you would have taken him in.'

'Yes, I would. However, he never came here, did he?'

'Maybe not. Can I ask for your cooperation with a list of the monks and their names? Their *real* names.' Monks left behind their birth name and entered the monastery, reborn, with a new Christian name. No surnames were used.

'Sorry, but no. We are not a part of your world, Captain, and we cherish our privacy. I have answered your questions and now I must be going. God's work awaits. Brother Rafael will escort you out,' he said and pointed to the monk standing behind the motionless Sergeant. Then, he turned and slowly strolled off through the lemon and orange trees.

'I could easily come back with a court order,' I shouted with slight anger mixed with several parts of annoyance.

'Raise your words, Captain. Not your voice. It is rain that grows the flowers, not the thunder,' he spoke up, but did not turn to face me. He continued his stroll, until he vanished into the citrus forest. I counted to ten, breathing through my nose, exhaling from the mouth. While my body temperature lowered down to normal, Brother Rafael had opened the gate and Galanos was already sitting in the car. I was sure this was the place. No way did Alex go to the other monasteries; though I did send cops to ask there, cops who later reported that no-one had recognized the man in question.

I marched past the monk and a murmur was heard. I had to quickly turn off every single one of my inner voices and focus to put the murmur into a sentence. The gate closed behind me. I stood there puzzled. What did the monk mean?

'Not all can be grown here!' That's what Rafael had said.

With the blessings of the silence provided by Jason -I speak when spoken to- Galanos, the sentence kept on playing on repeat in my mind's jukebox.

Not all can be grown here. Not ALL can be grown here. First, the monk spoke to me. Proof that something was going on there. Proof that Alex Panayiotou had been there. The monk was there during the whole conversation with the abbot. Second, they grew all kinds of fruit and vegetables. He could, also, be referring to their livestock. But, they ate fish and rice... they needed medication... hmm... electricity, phones...

'Jason?'

'Yes, Captain?'

'Do monks ever come down to the village and buy groceries and stuff?'

'No, sir. They never leave their monastery.'

'How do you think they attain fish, rice and various other stuff they may need?'

'Oh, the supermarket's owner's son is an altar boy. He brings them everything they need. But they do live with as little as possible. It is a brave choice to lock yourself away from the world.'

'Brave?'

'Well, yeah. They give up so much and pray for the rest of the world. Don't you agree, Captain?'

'I don't know, Jason. I prefer the Mother Teresa types; that live in the world and help out till they die. But hey, who am I to judge?'

He did not reply. He seemed to be processing my opinion, but made no remark.

'Show me the way to the supermarket.'

'It will be closed now. It's half past six; it closes at six.'

'Where does the family live? Don't they live in the village?'

'Yes.'

'Let's get going to their house then.'

We drove in silence, with the windows down. The cool, autumn breeze swirling around in the car. The air was so much purer than back in foggy-land Athens. An orchestra of crickets, mosquitos and birds replaced the radio.

We entered Kaki Vigla village through the one artery that connected the double digit population with the rest of the island. As with all villages in Greece, the only place with any sort of movement was the local coffee shop, known as the kafeneio. Every kafeneio around Greece was the same. Housed in an outdated building, begging for a splash of paint, traditionally decorated, filled with wooden chairs and as you entered, you lowered the average age to seventy.

Galanos drove by slowly, scanning the senior men that stopped playing cards and tavli, and turned to see the *foreigners*.

'The supermarket owner is not here,' he said and drove off to a small house at the end of the road. I smiled at the thought that he knew everybody on the island. Small communities would never work for me.

The last light of the day playfully bounced upon the house's front garden. Fully-blossomed, red and white roses were a treat to the eyes, while the Greek variety of the jasmine plant was a treat to the nose.

No *beware of the dog* sign.

I opened the freshly painted gate and walked up to the front door. All windows were shut. No response to the ringing of the bell. I cautiously walked around the house. The sound of the old lady from next door made me jump out of my skin. And I have thick skin.

She had crept behind me and shrilled, 'Who are you? This is not your house. Go! Get away! I'm calling the police!' she threatened and waved her walking stick at me.

'I am the police, calm down and...'

'Mrs. Ioannou?'

She turned to face Sergeant Galanos, calling her by her name.

'Jason? Little Jason. My Holy Mary, you have grown up well boy. How is your lovely mother?'

I stood aside, waiting patiently for the mindless chit-chat about various relatives to come to a halt. I had crossed my arms above my beer belly and opened my eyes wide, trying to catch the Sergeant's attention. The old lady continued with her interrogation about aunts and neighbors and sighed out loud every time Jason informed her that someone had passed away.

'May God bless their souls,' she said once again and finally Galanos caught a glimpse of me. Embarrassed for leaving me waiting and for forgetting his mission, he turned a nice shade of red.

'Mrs. Ioannou. Where is the Leontiou family?'

'They are away tonight. Had a christening on the mainland. Don't know if they are staying for the night, but he did say that the shop will be open first thing in the morning.'

'Do you know where the christening is?' I asked.

'No,' she snapped; her sweet tone used with Jason faded away. 'Just because I'm old, doesn't mean I know all the village's gossip!'

I threw my head back and laughed. 'Of course not. Good night, Mrs. Ioannou,' I said and walked off to the car.

'Good night to you. I'm not off to bed! Celebrity Games Night is on!'

She kissed Jason tenderly on his cheek and sent her regards to all his living relatives. At least I had a chance to see Jason smile.

'May God be with you,' she wished him and closed her net door behind her. Mindless commercials were still on.

We would have to wait until morning. *Wait.* One of my least favorite words in the English language. Now, I was the silent one.

'She is a good old lady, Mrs. Ioannou. She was my kindergarten teacher, my mother's too!'

I nodded and assumed a facial expression of '*really*?'

'I know many people can't wait to leave their villages and their islands to live on the mainland, in one of the big cities, but I love that I lived my whole life here. I know everyone and everyone knows me. People here are closer to their roots, their land, their church, and their traditions. And it is so close to Athens that I even stayed at home, while enrolled in the Academy.'

I smiled and wished him a good night as I parked beside his 90's, black Honda Civic that occupied the only parking slot belonging to the studio police station. I drove off in a hurry; twenty minutes left for the last ferry to Athens.

My heartbeat dropped as I drove onto the ferry with two whole minutes to spare. It was a sweet night. The fresh breeze mingled with the ocean's unique smell, the cloudless sky with its myriads of twinkling spots of light and the calm sea reflecting the almost full moon, ordered me to not stay locked in my car. It took only twenty minutes to the mainland and it was worth every minute spent on the ship's upper deck. Loud ship horns interrupted the squawking of the seagulls. Piraeus port was welcoming passenger ships carrying exhausted and hungover folk from their island vacations. Monstrous cargo ships were embarking alongside the shiny yellow forklifts waiting to upload long, metallic containers; their bellies filled with goods ranging from cars to cans of baked beans. The city shined bright, making you forget how tedious the concrete city really looked. It outshined the stars and polluted the environment, but it looked majestic and strangely peaceful. That is until, you drove into it and got stuck in traffic with the rest of the ants. This ant was hungry. This ant ordered from his local tavern, strapatsada for starters, lamb chops with lemon and oregano for the main course and baklava for dessert. Yes, this ant was hungry. The cook made strapatsada just how he liked it. Three eggs scrambled with olive oil, tomato puree and feta cheese.

I unlocked the screeching wooden door and entered my begging-for-a-clean, one bedroom apartment. I threw the bags of food onto my coffee table, fetched a knife, a fork and two ice cold Mythos beers from the kitchen, undressed down to my boxers, scratched my privates and fell back onto my black leather sofa. Dexter was just starting on Star Channel. Perfect. By the end of the suspenseful episode, all food was consumed and my eyes were growing heavy. Nirvana. Morpheus took over. The last thought of the day slid through my conscious mind...

Not all can be grown here...

Chapter Nine

He pushed open the heavy door. He felt even more excited than the time before, yet he did not show it. He was not alone this time. His Piggy did not lift up his head this time. For a moment he worried that *it* had died. Thankfully, his large belly gave away that he was breathing.

'Take him up,' he ordered. 'Wash him down with the hose. Be extra careful with the wings. Tie him up to the cross and gather the brothers. I'll be up shortly.'

He stood aside and started to pray. He watched as the four monks accompanying him carried out his orders. He fought back an evil smile. His Piggy found the strength to try to resist. He shook back and forth, but the strong hands holding him remained around his arms. All he achieved was to dirty the cell's floor with blood from his wounds and with his own filth that was stuck on him.

He watched them ascend the steps and waited until he was sure he was alone. He unlatched the bolt of the nearby cell. He stood in the doorway with the lit wall-candle behind him. He loved how his shadowy figure scared his prisoners. Especially the young ones. The little blonde girl ran and curled up in the corner. Her eyes, sore from the lack of light, revealed the fear being born across her pale face.

'Do not cry, little girl. We are killing Piggy tonight. If you're lucky we will be ready for you in a few days. Soon, you will go and meet all the other bastards this world has rightfully struck down!'

The little girl stood up and ran towards him begging him to let her go. She stretched out her little arms to hug his leg and implore him to show mercy. With a face of disgust, he lifted his right leg and kicked her hard in the chest, throwing her back against the cold stone wall.

'Do not touch me with your unholy bastard hands!'

He stepped back and slammed the door shut. He paused and touched his heart. He was getting too old for this. He had much to do and he was not sure how much longer the Lord would keep him on this Earth. He hastened up the steps and dashed to his chambers. He ran through the open door and knelt before the Holy Book. He rose with difficulty and bowed to kiss the book's animal-leather cover. He caught his breath and picked up the book, placing it with care between his body and his arm. He looked out of the oval window. Clean Piggy was tied up to his cross. Monks walked to and from him, gathering wood and placing it around him. Everything was set. He thanked God for His assistance and trudged down to the courtyard.

With the assistance of his brothers, he climbed the wooden ladder to the tiny balcony that jutted out of the wall, looking displaced. Similar to the many wildflowers that, against all odds, found a way to grow out of the stone wall.

He coughed to clear his throat, pulled out his small, reading glasses from his robe's lonely pocket and placed the heavy book on the balcony's thick wooden railing. As he fixed his glasses upon his broad Greek nose, the last monk had gathered below and all stood in formation. No one spoke. The only thing interfering with the silence was the rubbing of 'Piggy's' flesh against the chunky ropes that enclosed his arms and feet.

'My dear brothers... In the name of the Father, the Son and The Holy Spirit, I welcome you here tonight, in yet another step to fulfil our earthly mission. I will now read from the Gospel of our Lord, Jesus Christ.' In unison, all the monks knelt to the ground and lowered their heads.

'Coming forth, is the Antichrist! He who will rule for a thousand years, if not stopped in my name. Killed he can be, yet a ghost he is. Give him flesh and mortal he becomes. The Beast calls upon his demons. He opens a seal and the seal says kill the unjust, the liars, the hypocrites. Send them to me! And the demons yelled with joy. He opens a second seal and the seal says kill the filthy, the greedy, the swine that enjoy devouring the earth. Send them to me! And the demons yelled with joy. He opens a third seal and the seal says kill the bastards, the ones born of incest, of lust. Send them to me! And the demons yelled with joy. Finally, he opens a fourth seal. Send me murderers. And the demons yelled with joy. These souls do not enter Heaven. They are owned by the Beast. When he has received, he will appear in the flesh...' He stopped reading and all rose together. They turned and faced *Piggy*. Now, he could smile.

'Let light shine out of darkness!' he yelled, quoting from Corinthians.

Flames were born and wood started to crackle. The red

river of fire swallowed up the olive logs and grew into flaming lashes. *Piggy* was consumed in minutes.

The man contained his laughter and his desire to dance, as the sound of burning skin cracking and popping reached his ears. The flames danced in his wide open eyes. What a glorious night.

Chapter Ten

I awoke, startled by the excruciating rape of my ear. Dozens of too-happy-for-seven-in-the-morning people were screaming with joy, getting pumped up as they followed the enthusiastic fit gymnast of the Morning Show. I had forgotten that I had set my TV-alarm to go off.

Cold sweat covered my body. My last dream was Gaby's murder. My baby girl gunned down in the street. I also dreamt of Alex Panayiotou being stabbed over and over again; the downside of possessing a visual-spatial type of brain.

I lifted myself from the sofa and looked into my bedroom. My soft bed all made up, staring at me with complaint.

'I miss you too,' I whispered in my rough, barbarian morning voice.

On my way to the bathroom, I pulled down my boxers and kicked them to the smelly pile of dirty linen. I leaned my hands against the wall, closed my eyes and listened to my waterfall make contact with the bog's water. I hopped into the shower and let the man-made rain wash away all the dirt and all my thoughts. Nothing like a cold shower to get you going for the day.

I dried myself quickly and threw the wet towel onto the growing pile. I walked naked to my bedroom, opened my wardrobe and randomly picked out a pair of brown trousers, a white shirt and a brown suit jacket. I threw them on my bed and stared at myself for a moment in the full body mirror.

Am I letting myself go or is this what work and time does to you?

A running-out-my-wardrobe cockroach interrupted my thoughts. I swore for not wearing slippers and I swore again for cockroaches still being around this time of year. Who could blame them though? The rainy season seemed to be cancelled this year. It may still be warm enough for cockroaches, but thank God it wasn't enough for mosquitos.

Damn you, Noah. Mosquitos? Cockroaches? Really?

Half an hour later, I was walking into HQ for the chief's morning briefing, cockroach leftovers still stuck on my shoe. The chief enjoyed holding briefings first thing in the morning and watching everyone rush around trying to have a cup of coffee and get their shit together. Mercy for the officer who was not ready to answer any of his questions about ongoing cases.

'Good morning, Captain.' Sergeant Demetriou stood opposite me with her fiery red hair wrapped up in a bun.

'Good morning, Demetriou,' I replied, feeling bad for not knowing her first name. P.Demetriou, her name tag revealed. At her height, she had a good view of my once white shirt, now bearing evidence of my breakfast. A faint stain of coffee and a drop of honey from my baklava deco-rated it, just under the wrinkly collar. She pulled out a wet wipe and the smell of freshly cut lemons filled the air between us. Without asking, she wiped the two stains.

'It will dry in a minute. The chief is already behind the lectern.'

'Thanks...' I mumbled and rushed to catch the elevator's Symplegades from closing.

I pushed open the double glassed door and made a beeline for the front. A bunch of uniforms in their early thirties filled up the room, looking all serious and professional, hiding the fact that most of them were part hungover and part half-asleep. Yesterday, was Sergeant's Andreas - A.K.A. Party Animal- Triantafyllou thirty-fourth birthday and most of the force partied until the morning's first rays dug through the scattered clouds and reminded them that the night never lasts forever.

P.Demetriou passed before me and handed the chief a pile of reports and a few files.

'Thank you, Polina,' his gruff voice was heard. *Polina. That's it.*

Polina -previously known as P.Demetriou- sat down beside me.

'You missed a hell of a party,' she said, noticing me gazing at the stupid grins everybody was exchanging.

'Work...'

She smiled. 'All work and no play...'

'Settle down. Let's get things going. Mary?' the chief's deep voice echoed through the vast room.

Mary was already situated by the black Toshiba laptop that was connected to the room's projector. She flicked through images as the chief discussed the surge in car thefts. Captain Mike Michael stood up and gave the latest on his case. Then, closure on the murder of housewife Andrianna Katerchidou. Yes, the husband did it. The bank robbery was next, followed by the gang rape in Katexaki Park. The girl was only nineteen. *What a great city.*

'Salamina!' the lost-some-weight-lately chief announced and pulled me out of my thoughts about the sinful city.

'That is where most of you are going today!'

Everyone sat up straight, blinked a few times and cursed inside. Swearing for being wrong. Most were looking forward to a quiet day patrolling or even better with paperwork behind a desk. Their bodies craved for sleep and coffee.

'We have two people reported missing on the island and Captain Papacosta's murder case. You will split up into three teams. First team will go door to door in Salamina town where the five year old girl went missing, the other door to door in Aianteio village where our forty year old was last seen and the remaining team will search the area around the ditch where the murder victim was found. Now, Costa, Gianni take the mic, my fucking leg is killing me,' he grunted and plodded down the two steps and fell back into *his* chair. The black-suited silver head always sat in the same chair. It was the same as all the other chairs in the room, but it was his. And that's how he liked it. Without asking, Mary brought him over his second-for-the-day Greek coffee.

I nodded to Captain Gianni Antoniou to go first. His tree trunk legs shook the two wooden steps and we all got a view of his sweat forming a darker shade of grey, all down his back. He filled out his clothes to the point of no return. Undoubtedly, the biggest guy on the force. He laid his colossal hands on the lectern and his sausage fingers ran through his notes. He looked up. He owned a face that could inspire a cartoonist to create a masterpiece. Big round face, pointy ears, eyes too close to each other. However, to much surprise, he was quite the ladies' man. After his second divorce, he dedicated his efforts to pretty young Russian girls, much to the HQ's man power's envy. Every other Saturday, he would stroll into Odyssey Bar next to Head Quarters, introducing a Svetlana, a Tatyana or an Alina.

He cleared his sore tar-filled throat. A chain smoker since high school, Gianni was the type of guy that made me glad my daughter Gaby had persuaded me to quit smoking. Endless coughing, yellow teeth, sick-looking fingernails and a good ten years added to his face.

'Thomas Aristopoulou. Age 42. Big shot lawyer. His office is just down the road from here. Went to Salamina two days ago for business. In the village Aianteio. Hasn't been seen since.' Big Gianni always spoke like a telegraph when in front of an audience. Unless, he had a beer in one hand, a cigar in the other and was telling a rude sexist joke.

A well-presented youthful forty year old with blue eyes appeared on the wall screen opposite us. Overweight, but a good looking bloke who took care of himself. 'Reported missing by the wife, father of two primary school boys.' The projector clicked and ticked and a blonde little girl with faint freckles on her high cheekbones was smiling at us with a wide grin that revealed her missing teeth. 'Anna Mikropoulou. Age 5. Reported missing by her mother yesterday morning. Could have been gone all the previous night. They were staying at Salamis Bed and Breakfast. Two went to bed, one woke up there.' He cleared his throat again. 'You will each take the photo shown and turn every rock and tree, and knock on every door. Someone must have seen them. I will interview the mother again. Lieutenant Theodorou, you will be in charge of overseeing the search for the missing lawyer.'

'Aye Captain,' Theodorou stood up, nodded and sat back down.

Just as he lifted his right trunk to turn, I asked 'Is either case church related?'

The Captain processed my question as he turned back round. There was a slight rumble in the room, put to death by the chief's *be quiet* cough.

'How... erm.. How did you know?'

'Suspicion. So are they?'

'The lawyer was meeting with a client who was suing the church over land disagreements. His client claimed to own titles for land used by the church.'

The chief's eyes focused on me. Studying me. Trying to get inside my head.

'And the mother of the missing girl?' I continued.

'When I interviewed her, she had a priest with her. She said he was her pneumatiko, her spiritual father. She came to Salamina to confess.'

'Confess what?'

'Having a child out of wedlock.'

'I see...' and my mind's engine went into overdrive.

I was up next. Alex Panayiotou. His brutalized face appeared on the white wall. I walked them through the case; what the mother said, what the boss said, the coroner, the monastery. I described the area where the body was found. I read disappointed faces of sleepless officers, realizing that they would be spending their day under the sun, on a hill slope, looking in the bushes, bagging pieces of rubbish. I presented them with my awkward I-am-done smile and wished them a good day. I fell back into my chair, words and pictures swirling around the corners of my mind.

The chief stood up and ordered everybody to their duties. They all scattered like cockroaches when the lights got switched on. Mary and her laptop left last. As the door shut behind her hourglass figure, the chief came and sat down beside me. He did not say a word. His method of getting things out of you. He did not even look at you. He just sat there until you spoke. A method he used in his prime days as a homicide investigator, back when people were arguing about who was better. Michael Jackson or Prince?

'I know you hate hunches. I know you hate it when I say a have a feeling about this. But, come on, when was the last time Salamina ever had a murder and two disappearances in a matter of days? Never, that's when. And that abbot. Oh, I don't trust that abbot. And I am sure, even though without evidence, that Alex was there. I need a warrant to enter the place.'

'No judge will give you a warrant to search a monastery, especially based on a *feeling.*' He mocked the last word.

'No, but any judge would give *you* a warrant.'

He smiled. 'I like your balls Papacosta, but go get me some evidence, any evidence, and I'll get you your warrant.'

Not all can be grown here...

Chapter Eleven

Car. Port. Ferry.

Little police station on the prairie.

You know the drill.

Presentable Jason was waiting outside. A wrapped package, held tight, was under his right armpit. *Floral pink wrapping paper?* The present was not from him. He hopped in the car.

'Good morning, Captain. Lovely day today, is it not? Though it should rain one of these days; the crops need their water. How are you today, Captain?'

So you talk when nervous. I decided to put him out of his misery.

'Your mum sent me a present?'

He went from a blush to a mature tomato red.

'You are indeed a great detective. Yes, she knitted you a cover for your coffee table.'

He passed me the neatly wrapped package and turned beetroot red.

'Thank her dearly from me. And stop being embarrassed. Greek mothers must do what Greek mothers do!'

Red boy and Grinning Captain drove through the countryside discussing rural villages and their rustic way of life in the bucolic setting. The mountains that made up our horizon were cloaked in green and their peaks shrouded in white clouds. Clouds, but no rain. A November acting like a September.

We arrived in Kaki Vigla and took the only two-way road the village had. Papageorgiou supermarket was open for business. Hopefully, their son would be in, too.

I pulled up in one of the six white-painted rectangles that served as the store's parking lot. Two elderly ladies were exiting the store, wheeling behind them their groceries for the week. Green veggies sprouted out of their bags, as they complained about sore feet and drowsiness from their new prescription pills.

'Oh, I hate these new yellow pills!'

'Perhaps you're not supposed to take them with your pink pills. What did the doctor say?' her friend with more moles than teeth asked.

'He just gives me pills and says "one every morning-evening-night" and sends me on my way. At ninety-two, I think he doesn't expect me to be back, but there I am every month to fill up my stock of colorful pills! I have enough to make a rainbow!'

They both laughed. Humor. Best medicine available. And with that thought, we entered the quite-large-for-a-village grocery.

'It serves all the nearby villages,' Jason declared, having read the look on my face as I gazed at the variety-filled aisles. His voice intruded the Greek hits of the eighties that echoed through the store. Golden oldies flowing out through creak-ing, once white speakers that hung in all four corners of the vast shop. In the right hand corner was a counter where ciga-rettes and magazines were sold. An office space was visible behind it. A man stood there, studying delivery reports, his eyes moving rapidly behind thick black reading glasses. He had the moustache of a past-era porn star which was lifted by a friendly smile that welcomed us as we approached.

'Mr. Papageorgiou, I am Jason Galanos...'

'Oh, Demetris's son...yes.'

'We are here on a police matter. This is Captain Papa-costa. He needs to ask your son a few questions.'

His smile dropped and his bushy grey eyebrows met.

'Nico? What has Nico done? He is a good boy...'

'He did not do anything, sir. Relax. I just need to ask him if he saw a man who has been reported missing.'

He studied me for a second, with that disapproving look villagers give strangers that they do not trust.

'Wait in the office.' He nodded to the open door behind him. 'I'll go and get my son.'

We both sat on the magnolia two-seater that began from one wall and ended on the next. Opposite us was a desk filled with papers and accounting books and family photos sealed away in shiny frames. A small coffee table filled the room between the sofa and the desk; a coffee table that soon hosted two ice cold, homemade lemonades, a plate of chocolate filled biscuits and a plate filled of watermelon pieces swimming in honey flavored syrup. Greek hospitality provided by the owner's wife who entered with a forced smile and a worried look. She wished us a good day, left the plastic tray and rushed back to work.

Just as bitter lemon froze my upper lip, Mr. Papageor-giou ushered in a sixteen year old boy; holding him firmly by the shoulders. The boy had messed-up brown hair and wore a weird grin that revealed his needing-a-brush braces.

'This is Nico. Nico say hi,' he told the boy as if he was talking to a toddler.

'Hi,' the teen said and giggled.

'I am Captain Papacosta...'

'Hi,' he said and giggled again.

'Is something amusing you?'

'Don't get him wrong. Nico is a special boy. He is always happy.' The father explained to me in a subtle way, what I later read in the boy's school file. Nico was never going to progress mentally past the age of five. I showed him the photograph of Alex Panayiotou and asked if he had seen the man before. He shook his head from side to side to state a no.

'Thank you for your time,' Jason stood up.

I then flashed the boy the photograph of the missing girl, much to Jason's surprise. Again the violent shaking of the head. Next was the lawyer's photograph.

'No, no, never seen Piggy.'

'Now, Nico. That isn't very nice, is it? Are we done, Captain?'

I stood up, mechanically shook his hand and walked out the office; disappointed. I picked up a pack of Marlboro Gold and a cheap lighter, threw a ten Euro note on the counter and exited the supermarket. Jason found me with one of my gluteus maximus on the car's warm hood. I took a long drag, making the newly-lit cigarette's end turn into an orange-tipped flame. I let the smoke swirl around my lungs before releasing the air through my nose.

'Whose were those photos...'

'Don't you ask me shit, boy. You know these people. Why the heck did you not tell me that Nico was *not all there*?'

He paused. He wore an expression hard to read. He seemed to be counting. He reminded me of my anger-management uncle Phil. Counting to ten to relax was his panacea. *Okay, so you're angry too!*

'Sir, with all due respect, Nico is an excellent young man, capable of answering a simple *have you seen this man* question! And he is all there! He is as God made him, he plays basketball, he likes music...'

I lifted my palm, asking him to stop.

'I'm sorry, Jason. You are not to blame. Nico is not to blame either.' More smoke. 'The photos are of two missing people, last seen here on the island.'

'Really? First time I am hearing about this...'

'Neither was reported missing to the police here in Salamina, but in Athens. The lawyer's wife went to her local police station and the girl's mother called central. Anyway, let's get going to check up on the search party.'

I drove slowly through the strikingly picturesque village; left mostly untouched since Greece had a king. I could see Nico in my rear view mirror, speeding along on his black mountain bike with grocery bags on each side of the handlers. He zoomed pass us, singing: 'Piggy's gonna burn, piggy's gonna burn, la la la lala, piggy's gonna burn!'

'Piggy. That's what he called the lawyer!' I stepped on the gas, overtook the cheery adolescent and came to a tire-screeching halt. I got out and ran to block his way.

'Nico, Nicoooo,' I called him to me.

He froze in front of me, his trembling eyes looking up into mine.

'Who told you Piggy's going to burn?'

He looked left and right and shivered, realizing he was alone on the street with me. I raised my voice.

'Who told you Piggy is going to burn? Answer me!'

Tears started to fall. 'Sir?' Jason asked, standing by the car's open door.

'Tell me,' I yelled.

'No! No! I can't! I can't! I can't!'

'Why Nico? Why can't you tell me?'

'The abbot said no police.' The words fell out between the awkward giggles.

'The abbot?' I let go of his bike's rubber handlebars and let him pedal off to the old lady who ordered the groceries.

I knew it!

'Come on, come on... Pick up... Chief! It's Papacosta. It's the abbot. The kid recognized the lawyer. We need a warrant quick; they could still be alive!'

Chapter Twelve

The last sunrays of the day had sunk into the ocean. Orange and red waves by the horizon turned dark blue. The night rolled in. The mountains around us silent and black. The flickering blue lights from the horde of police cars, flashing round and round, making shadows dance across the hills. Like a slithering snake, the line of patrol cars headed up the narrow dirt road towards the gloomy monastery. One after the other, the cars came to a standstill as armed policemen exited them and prepared to storm into the building.

The gate was open. Inside only darkness; quiet as a grave. The light had left and taken the wind with it. I went in first, gun steady between both my hands, flashlights from the men and women behind me showing me the way through inky trees that stood similar to soldiers under inspection. The smell of smoke reached us, blended with the ghastly odor of burnt flesh. Suddenly, we were faced with an image none of us would ever be able to remove from our minds. Every circle of light revealed a body.

Cloaked in brown, all you could see was their faces. Hollow eyes, mouth violently wide open, all facial muscles stretched and distorted. Blood dripping from their noses formed crimson rivers upon their dead faces. The lights moved around. Bodies everywhere. Small see-through vials lay on the concrete ground in front of them.

Poison.

Polina located the main switch and the overhead spotlights came to life. We all froze at the sight of the smoking charcoal body glued to the stake by burning skin. His mouth screaming out without flesh to cover his teeth. The fire had burned so hot, it reached his bones.

If this was the lawyer...

'Find the girl! Find the girl! Look everywhere!' Half the force scattered through the trees or entered the cells and church. The other half checked the bodies for signs of life. Twenty two dead and counting.

The abbot's body was crouched over a thick leather covered book. He had decorated it with his bloody saliva; his wrinkly fingers holding on tight. I wore my latex gloves and, finger by finger, I removed the heavy book from his grasp. Could this be the gospel of Christ? I carefully placed it in a large evidence bag and called over Polina Demetriou. Someone I could trust. I ordered her to get it quickly back to our labs and notify the chief. He would know what experts to call in. She managed a faint smile upon her ashen face and sped off to carry out her task.

They knew we were coming...

'I avoid such sweet *temptations*... The supermarkets owner's son is an *altar boy*... It is a *brave* choice to lock yourself away from the world... I love that I lived my whole life here. *I know everyone and everyone knows me.* People here are closer to their roots, their land, their *church*, their traditions...

He is as *God* made him,' Jason's voice echoed out of the darkest parts of my mind. He never spoke to the monks. He grew up close to the church. He mentioned Nico was an altar boy, but made no reference to his situation. He was nervous whenever we drove up to the monastery or talked about the monks. I turned and searched for Sergeant Galanos. He stood motionless as a statue, unable to come forward and accept the images his eyes were receiving. I walked slowly towards him, noticing silent tears running freely down his cheeks.

'You okay?'

No reply.

'Captain! We have her! We found her! She's alive!'

'Get the paramedics here fast! She has been poisoned!'

Sergeant Mikropoulos held a police blanket in his arms. Blonde hair spilt out the top. Two small scared blue eyes were gazing through the darkness. That is when I heard Galanos move. I spun around in a heartbeat to see him, pointing his firearm towards the girl. I blocked his view.

'Move out the way, Captain or I will blow your head wide open. The girl must die or everyone's death will be in vain!'

'She is a five year old little girl!'

'She is a bastard! We need a dead bastard for the prophecy. Now, move!'

His yelling made heads turn and guns were pulled out.

'Jason, please. Lower your gun....'

'Shut it! You know nothing! We could have defeated the Antichrist. Oh, don't you all look at me like I am crazy. It is all in the book of our Savior! You will see, when you read it! With their deaths, they would have completed the four seals! The girl should have died!'

'She didn't like the horrid soup she was served, you

fucking freak,' Sergeant Mikropoulos spat out with disgust. The girl had taken one sip and left the rest of the soup untouched. The monks had failed.

Jason looked around him. The hate on the faces staring back at him. Guns ready to send him to meet his maker.

'When you are ready, my child, come and find me,' he quoted from the so-called Gospel of Christ and put his gun in his mouth.

'Nooo,' I yelled, but my voice was drowned out by the gunshot that put a hole through Jason's skull, sending parts of his brain into the air and coloring the lemon tree behind him with stains of fresh blood. His body fell to the dirt, bringing the total body count to thirty-five. Thirty-three monks, a lawyer and a poor boy that had his head screwed up and turned into scrambled eggs.

It took all night to tag and bag the bodies. We needed two morgues to store them all.

The first ray of sun travelled through the darkness and put an end to the nightmare of a night. It found me, up high on the police ferry, wiping away a lonely tear. The morning breeze was not strong enough to take away the smell of death that covered the boat. We all helped the paramedics load the bodies into the ambulances lined up along the pier. All major news outlets were set up, held back by a thin yellow tape dancing in the wind. Serious looking, smart talking, well dressed people stood in front of cameras and described the scene. Shots of flashing cameras echoed across the port and newspaper reporters shouted questions to anyone in uniform.

In a zombie-like state, we all got into our patrol cars, drove back to Headquarters, took a shower -some two- and headed to the canteen for breakfast. No one spoke a word.

We ate in silence. No one left until I dragged myself up and pushed open the glass door.

On my desk, just as I had requested, the files of the monks' history. Birth certificates, medical reports, past convictions, everything. All the puzzle pieces quickly fell together. The abbot, known outside of the monastery's walls as Giannis Keraunos, had mental issues and suffered from violent outbursts since primary school. A great leader, indeed.

Five monks were left-handed.

They all stabbed Alex once, making them all murderers.

Jason's file was there too. Straight A student, role model in his society; I pushed all the files onto the floor. My computer took a flight out of the open window and met the parking lot below.

Chapter Thirteen

DR. ARIADNE METAXA'S OFFICE

'And that is how I ended up being forced to talk to you!'

'So, according to their holy book, if the girl died, the Antichrist would arrive? I'm confused. Is that something they wanted?'

'After explaining the four seals, the book went to reveal specific ways to kill the Antichrist. Anyway, it was all just a bunch of bull. The book has been dated to 1200 A.D. Even if it was copied from an earlier book, experts have singled out words in the text that were not used during Jesus' lifetime. The monks were misled by a psycho who enjoyed killing.'

Dr. Ariadne scribbled down a few lines in her purple notebook and looked up at me.

'So the denouement of the case came at a terrible cost.'

'The what?'

'The resolution of the mystery.'

'Are we back to talking about closure? Yes, I have accepted my faults, Jason's death and I have moved on.'

'You sure about that, Captain?'

I smiled. 'As sure as I am about most things.'

More scribbling in her notebook.

'Don't forget your water,' she reminded me for the third time with her mellifluous voice. She had one rule. While in session, her patients had to drink a minimal of four full glasses of room temperature water. Apparently, it helped the mind. My mind yearned for beer during hot days and whiskey during the cold ones. The ice in my whiskey was made of water, but I doubt Dr. Ariadne would approve of my habits. I drank my water and gazed out of the glass wall. The port was in full swing. It was a funny sensation to see all the commotion, yet not hear a single sound.

'22nd of December today,' she said and, as always, I could sense her eyes reading me.

'Yes, a Monday,' I commented, avoiding the question behind her statement.

She smiled that unique smile only seen by mothers when they hear something clever from their smart-ass offspring.

'How are you spending Christmas, Captain?'

Flashes from last year's pitiful Christmas spawned and played like a trailer in my inner home theatre. Me and a bunch of divorced guys from work at Archontiko Bar, eating pub food and drinking cheap beer.

'Home, alone. Not really one for festivities.'

'It is a good time to unwind and replace horrid images with other ones more pleasant.'

'If I manage to wake up early, I might go to church. Sit there for a while, then grab a meal and head home.'

'Do you find going to church helpful?'

'I think I go out of habit. My mother, like most Greek mothers, woke us up every Sunday and took us. Now I do my best to make it on the *important* dates. You?'

It was the first time I had asked her a personal question.

'Oh, I'm an Atheist. No higher powers out there for me. But, professionally speaking, I must admit that in specific cases, church going has helped with patients of mine. I love cooking for everyone on Christmas. A few family members and a couple of close friends...'

'How very Hannibal Lecter of you!' I joked and managed to hear the doctor's unique laughter. A very restrained laughter, but still laughter.

'You should join us...' Her eyes were reading me again.

'Do you invite all your patients to parties?'

'No, just the special ones.'

'I'll think about it. Thank you.'

Thunder swallowed my last words and lightning drew our attention to the outside world. Soon, fat raindrops were falling in their thousands. We sat in silence, admiring nature. She enjoyed the rain as much as I did.

Chapter Fourteen

The phone would not stop ringing.

It felt like hours had passed as my arm searched for my bedside table. My cell phone provided the only light in my dark bedroom.

'Hello?' More of a grunt than a word.

'Good morning, Captain and a happy fucking new year to us both!'

'Ioli?' I sat up. Her laughter echoed in my ears as I rubbed my deprived of sleep; black bagged eyes.

'It's eleven o'clock. Thought you were an early bird.'

'Not when I get home at five in the morning!'

'Well, well, well... Look who's living the wild life in the big city!' Her annoying *nudge* managed to find its way to my shoulder -even over the phone.

'Shut up! I was down at the bar with the rest of the no-where-better-to-go rejects from the station, just like I did on Christmas. You?'

'Enjoyed time with my family and friends. I'm coming tomorrow... to Athens, for good,' she stressed each word, still trying to persuade herself that it was happening for real. After the Olympus Killer, she was promoted to Lieutenant A' and officially my partner; our team was in charge of homicide investigations over the Greek islands.

'You ready?'

'As I'll ever be! Everything has already been shipped to my new apartment in Athens, my suitcase is packed and my mother is preparing me with enough meals to last me well into the next ice-age.'

'So, I guess I'll be seeing you tomorrow then!'

'Yes, sir. Ready for duty,' she said and the phone went silent.

I sat up, feeling like some damn woodpeckers had just moved into my frontal lobe.

In Chania, Crete, Ioli was not feeling much better. She stood alone in her now empty apartment, her thoughts bringing tears to her eyes.

Ioli never cared much about housework. She never understood the joy her mother and aunts talked about when they had finished all their chores; their pride of a spotless house after a full day of cleaning and tidying up.

Her apartment was not dirty, yet she never dedicated much effort to keeping it tidy. She saw it as a place to shower, sleep and get dressed before going back to work. Now, empty before her eyes, she realized she would miss her one-bedroom home.

A new chapter awaited her. Her gunshot wound had healed and mentally she felt ready to catch some bad guys. She lived for the investigation process. She was born for it. The youngest Lieutenant at 32 and now at 35 Lieutenant A'.

'Goodbye home,' she whispered and locked the door behind her.

Chapter Fifteen

CASE NO.2: THE RED HORSE - ENDING
PEACE, PEOPLE KILLING ONE ANOTHER...

Kate -Katerina- Spanou awoke in her four-bedroom, blue and white painted, country house on a fine winter morning. Santorini may be one of the top destinations in the summer, but Kate loved it during the winter. The peace in the air, the majestic sunsets over the ocean, the now stressed-free locals, finally relaxing after a long and exhausting summer season working in hotels, bars, restaurants, water sports, souvenir shops and other services provided for the tourists that flocked to the island during hot months.

She woke alone. Her husband Mario had been gone for hours. She never understood why fishing had to start so early.

Saturday mornings were always peaceful. Her two daughters stayed with her mother on Fridays and they all met up Sunday morning at church, after which the girls returned home.

She sat down at her round wooden kitchen table and bit down on her honey-covered toast. Nothing signaled that today was the day that she planned to kill her husband.

Today was an ideal day to kill him, with the kids gone and Mario out fishing. Even the chicken had defrosted to its core, ready for their midday romantic meal. She cleaned the house through and through, chopped up the potatoes and the homegrown carrots, had a nice, hot shower and wore *that* dress Mario loved to see on her. She poured herself a glass of chilled white wine and cropped the vegetables around the chicken that sat alone in the Pyrex. A quarter of a liter of olive oil and a handful of salt later and Mario's final meal was ready for the oven. She sat back, drank the remaining wine down in one long gulp and waited.

One o'clock and the front door finally opened. Mario came smiling in, five or six fish tangling dead from his hand. His smile widened at the sight of the black dress that revealed her bare left shoulder. The smell of roasted chicken filled the narrow hallway. He stood opposite his petite wife and bend down to kiss her with passion on her thin lips.

'Mmm, something smells nice.'

'And you stink of fish,' she joked and pulled back playfully.

'Give me ten minutes,' he said, kissed her again with force and ran up the stairs.

Kate knew she was not a *pretty girl*. Short, always a few kilos heavier than she would have preferred, pale skin, hook-like nose and boring eyes. She knew people thought her lucky to have a man like Mario. Tall, athletic, handsome, with dark, seductive eyes and a magazine front-page smile. She felt insecure at first, but after their perfect wedding day and two beautiful daughters, she was living the family dream.

'But, men will be men... and men are pigs!' she whispered to herself as she served their portions.

Mario gobbled down her delicious offering and then

asked for dessert in a playful tone. She giggled and ran up the steps, jumping on their king sized bed. He chased her; his clothes falling to the floor one by one. He was completely naked by the time he reached their door. He stood there, breathing heavily, like an animal ready to attack and devour her. She pulled up her dress, to reveal that no underwear graced her body. Soon, he was on top of her, kissing her violently along her neck. She moaned into his ear and he entered her with *that joy* that men feel as their favorite toy finds refuge in a warm wet vagina. He pulled up her dress, over her head and threw it to the floor. His tongue journeyed down and reached her breasts.

He bit her nipples. He knew all her buttons.

'Did Stella and Maria love having their nipples bit?'

His body froze, his erection started going soft, his eyes were painted with terror.

'Baby, I... What rumors have you been...'

'Oh, don't baby me,' she said with disgust and pushed him off her.

He stood up and started to mumble words of apology that fell dead upon reaching Kate's ears. She looked at the clock.

'Shut up! Screw your lies. And please, get off my Persian carpet. Go die in the hallway!'

'Baby, they meant nothing, you are the one... Wait, what? Die?'

'Poison should kick in by now.'

It took him a minute of observing her face to realize she was serious. 'You bitch, you would poison your own husband? The father of your children?' The last word came with a cough. He felt his heart being stepped on by a stampeding elephant. An inner force pushed him to his knees. He then fell like a tree in free fall to the cold ground.

'Help...me...' the words were squeezed out from insides switching off.

'Your funeral will be great. I will even invite your girlfriends. Help enough?'

Chapter Sixteen

Three days later, Kate kept her promise. The funeral took place in Mario's village, Megalochori (Big Village). Everyone came to say goodbye to the forty year old that had died so young from a heart attack. Not many were surprised. Mario always had a weak pumper in his chest. The doctor had arrived at his house to find a crying, distraught Kate explaining how Mario felt chest pains during their *intimate moments* and how in a matter of seconds he had collapsed to the floor. He declared Mario dead, called Kate's mother to come comfort her and arranged the body's transfer to the morgue. No foul play, no police.

Agioi Anargyroi church in the center of the picturesque village soon filled up with tragic black dressed figures. His devastated mother, his grieving sister, his wife with two young girls in her arms, his friends and of course Stella and Maria, who both did an excellent job at hiding their sorrow. Both were married, yet the loss of a lover is painful. Their exciting dalliance had come to an abrupt end.

After the ceremony, they all followed the coffin to its

final resting ground. Through the narrow streets, past neoclassical houses, under the famous bell tower with the six bells forming a pyramid, along the side of grape-less vineyards and into the cemetery; a freshly dug grave waited for them, amongst white and grey marbled headstones. The wind blew strong and cold; the sunlight was scarce. Even the January sky had dressed in black.

'The view is to die for,' Katie joked to Mario, last time they were there, at an uncle's burial.

Just like in her hometown, the capital Thira, the cemetery clung to the top of the 400-meter cliff, looking down the caldera and into the blue waters that caressed the volcanic islands sleeping in the vast ocean.

Kate held her girls every second of the ordeal, only letting go when she approached the deep hole in the ground, looked down at Mario's coffin and as tradition ordered, she threw a handful of soil on top. As she walked away, men from the church and of the family picked up old shovels and proceeded to cover the hole.

Flowers were laid on top by the women and everyone walked back to his mother's house for coffee, biscuits and stories about the goodness in Mario's weak heart.

The next morning, Kate woke up once again in an empty house. The girls had stayed with her mother. Everyone agreed that she needed rest.

She had cried herself to sleep the night before. She did not regret her actions, but felt sorrow for her girls. Movie reels from happier days played through her mind, keeping her company until she finally managed to close her eyes and drift off to sleep.

Thoughts that woke up with her. Thoughts erased with a good strong Greek coffee and two slices of homemade bread with honey. Thunder also helped clear her mind. She got up, walked over to the kitchen window and opened it slowly. Drops of light rain flew in, but she did not mind. The smell of fresh air, fused with hints of sea water perfume, filled the spacious kitchen and entered her lungs. A little smile was born across her face.

'Life goes on...' she said out loud, the sentence coming at the end of an inner pep talk. It did, but not for Kate. The bullet flew through the rain and struck her in the face, just below her right eye. She was dead before she hit the icy floor. Her mother found her, the following morning, lying in a pool of blood. Her favorite cat sat beside her, enjoying a drink at the bloody pond, until he ran out the open window, chased out by the old lady's high pitched screaming.

Chapter Seventeen

Ioli Cara's arrival at Headquarters easily became the hot gossip of the first week of the new year. The arrival of a tall, athletic, young, single Cretan woman with long, black hair, dark, seductive eyes, sun-kissed skin and an amazing field record, fed hope to single and divorced cops in their thirties and minor envy to women who took time to accept foreign bees into the hive.

Ioli's outspoken character mixed with her love for food and a good time helped her adapt in an otherwise competitive playing field. I watched her as she walked confidently towards my desk, coffees in hand.

'Good morning, Captain,' she smiled, passing me my coffee and parking her jean wearing behind on the edge of my desk.

It is hard to explain the bond between partners who have lived through life-threatening danger together. I had saved her life from the hands of the Olympus Killer and she saved mine from boredom, depression and decay.

'Any murders today?'

I nearly spilt my coffee at the question. She flashed her trademark Julia Robert's smile and rushed to say 'You know what I mean. I don't wish people to die, but I have been here two weeks now and all I have been doing...'

'Is doing my paperwork,' I said, and passed her a couple of handwritten reports for her to type into the system.

She grabbed them, got up, looked at my office phone and ordered it to ring. Silence. Mumbling, she made her way to her desk. The neatest desk on the floor. She had even Blu-tacked her keyboard and her pencil holder down.

Polina Demetriou coughed behind me. She had brought more reports from the guys working Athen's homicides. I was starting to regret offering to help them with their workload. I meant with field work, not their paperwork.

'Erm, Captain, it is... erm..' she played with her curly hair and continued to inform me that it was Euaggelia's, the canteen lady's birthday and most were going to surprise her at closing time with a cake and beers. She asked me to join them.

'Yeah...' was the only word I managed to say. The roaring of my black old fashioned cheap telephone intruded upon my flow of thought.

'Captain Papacosta... Hmmm... Okay... Aha... Yes, setting off now.'

'Polina, call the police speedboat. Tell the driver to be ready in twenty minutes. Fuel up for Santorini.'

'Right away, sir.'

I stood up and crashed into Ioli, who was hovering around me.

'Dead woman, found in her home by her mother. Shot through the open window. She buried her husband yesterday,' I spoke in police telegraph talk as we made a beeline for the elevator doors.

'Kids?'

'Don't know.'

'Sad to lose both parents in a matter of days.'

We exited the underground parking, with its bad lighting and its smell of stagnant, stale air, carrying aromas of rubbish and cigarette smoke. Ever since smoking had been banned in all public buildings, it seemed like everyone lived in the basement or the roof.

'I'll drive,' Ioli said beeping open our patrol car. The one and only patrol car belonging to the Island's Homicide Department. In the back, my black and yellow Goodyear suitcase next to her double the size, red Samsonite, already packed since last week.

Chapter Eighteen

Four hours later, our ferry floated at the bottom of the 400 meter cliff. The blue lagoon between Santorini and the volcanic island opposite it, lay vacant. In the summertime, some of the largest cruise ships in the world stopped here releasing thousands for a day excursion. There are three ways up to Thira, walk the long, winding, labyrinthine road with the 600-plus steps, hire a donkey to carry you up (poor animals) or use the newly installed teleferic. We opted for the cable car.

'Santorini is the most beautiful Greek island, hands down,' Ioli declared, looking out the window; wires flying us up into the grey, winter sky.

'Couldn't agree more,' I answered, remembering another life, years ago, when as a young man, I came here from New York with my now ex-wife.

A young police constable welcomed us to the island. We walked through well-maintained, rock-paved roads towards the first parking lot. Driving was not possible along the edge of the precipice. A few shops were open, with a couple of postcard stands outside their door, but most were shut, with that polite little notice hanging on the door. CLOSED FOR THE WINTER.

The crackling in the skies above gave pace to our walk and as soon as our seat belts had us buckled in, the first drops made their way back down to earth.

Constable Christina Dionysiou informed us that the house of the late Kate Spanou, age 38, was just a few minutes away, located in a side road just after the church of Saint Minas.

'Her mother discovered the body. She was in a right state, sir, but I managed to take her statement. No idea what-so-ever about who would want to hurt her *precious angel*,' Christina said, passing me a piece of paper with a few drops of rain on it.

'How did her husband die?' Ioli beat me to the question.

'Heart attack. Always had a weak heart. A good man, Mario was. Loved in our small society.'

'His wife?'

'She kept to herself. Housewife, busy with chores and kids. Most described her as friendly and quiet.'

We parked outside the typical Greek island village house with the rose garden in front and a bricked pathway leading to the main entrance. Crying relatives and nosy neighbors had gathered and were contained under a yellow car-less parking tent by a tall muscular constable, all avoiding the heavy downpour. Constable Christina said something about an umbrella in the back, but before she had finished her sentence, Ioli and I were out of the car, dashing through the rain.

A long-in-the-tooth, grizzled and decrepit man stood in the hallway, looking at us; disapproving our entrance.

'Wipe your feet,' the eighty-year-old man growled. 'This way.'

'I see, coroners do not retire here,' Ioli whispered.

'More like a doctor who is enjoying government benefits and refuses to give up his throne.'

We followed him into the cold kitchen. The window was wide open, welcoming in the chilling air and a spray of rain fall. The woman's body was lying on the floor; an open wound in the middle of her face. A halo of blood formed around her. Blood spatter painted on the wall behind her and to her right.

'She stood right here,' Ioli said and stood by the kitchen sink and stared outside. 'Bullet came flying through the open window...'

'It looks like a bullet from a hunting rifle. The killer could not have stood at a long distance,' I said.

'The roof of the house opposite, otherwise he -or she- wouldn't have a clear shot.' She turned around holding a picture frame. A photograph of a four-member family, smiles all around, having fun at the beach. Ioli always felt for the children. 'They are never to blame and always get screwed over by an adult's bullshit,' she once told me.

'Are you two going to keep standing around or can I take the body now? I've been here for four hours!'

'Time for your meds?'

'What did you say, girl?'

'Yes, you can take the body... after you tell us the estimated time of death,' I intervened.

'Sometime yesterday morning; can't be dead for more than 24 hours. I'll know more after my apprentice performs the autopsy.'

I helped the doctor and his youthful apprentice with lifting up the body and placing it on the stretcher brought in by Kyriako a.k.a. old man's apprentice. Ioli went upstairs to look through the house for clues. I took the ground floor.

The body was wheeled outside and neither the muscular constable nor the torrential rain could hold back her mother and friends. They escorted their loved one to the back of the ambulance; their tears becoming one with the cloudburst.

We searched through private items, unfolding the life of a typical family. Photos from vacations, school clothes, jewelry, books, souvenirs, candles, socks, USBs, DVDs, gold-fish, ashtrays, perfumes, toys, piggy banks and the list went on. Pieces of materials that form our possessions. Pieces of a greater puzzle called domestic life.

The rain outside decided on a break. The black sky was rumbling loud, getting ready for round two. We discussed our findings on our way across the wet slippery road to the neighbor's doorbell.

Please not a grumpy, uncooperative senior. Ding-dong.

The door flew open in a split second.

'Yes?' the pink-haired twenty year old asked, trying to catch her breath. She had been watching from behind ripped worn-in beige curtains. Her cigarette lying in the tinted glass bowl that served as an ashtray, was still breathing out smoke into the untidy room, its furniture from another era. She was wearing a wide silly grin, jean shorts as wide as my belt, black socks to knee level and a white T-shirt with some club's logo printed on it. A T-shirt that did not leave much to the imagination.

'I am Lieutenant Ioli Cara, and this is Captain Papa-costa. We are here concerning the death of your neighbor, Katerina Spanou. Did you hear or see anything suspicious yesterday?'

'Err, nope. Nothing. I work nights, at Franco's bar and I sleep till evening after I get home.'

'Did you hear a loud noise like a gunshot while you slept?'

'Nah...' she scratched the shaved side of her head. 'I sleep with my headphones on. Can't sleep in quiet.'

'You live alone?'

'Yeah, this was my granny's house. She left it to me, so I thought, fuck it. I left Larissa and moved here. Found a job...'

'What ways are there to go up to your roof?' I asked.

'Just the one. From the ladder at the back of the house.'

'Mind if we take a look?'

'No freaking way! You think the bitch got shot from my roof? Wow, of course you can have a look.'

'Bitch, hey?' Ioli looked at her.

'Not that I had anything to do with the lady. She did not like me much. She was always looking at me funny.'

'What about her husband?'

'Mario? He was okay, I guess. Rather handsome for his age. But I don't like ladies' men. I might be a bar-woman, but I'm not a player.'

'And Mario was?' I asked.

'Yeah, wife at home and there he is with that Stella woman from the grocery store.'

'And what grocery store is this?'

'At Karouanos.'

We walked round the side of the house and took a look at the old rusty ladder that led to the top of the house. The yard's fence was ruined along most parts. Anyone could have just walked in and gone up the ladder.

'Ioli, go tell Constable Christina and Hercules to go round the neighborhood asking if anyone saw or heard anything. Find out where Karaounos is and meet me at our car. Let's go visit this Stella.'

'How about port checks and planes?'

'I don't think planes fly here during the winter. International, that is. Maybe a weekly flight to Athens. Check it. We could send a message to the ports, for them to be alert and check people's IDs and reason for traveling, but no way the chief would agree on a lockdown.'

She nodded in agreement and walked off. My eyes made sure Ioli had turned out of sight.

'Can I have a cigarette?'

'Sure, policeman dude. She your lady or something?' the girl asked, taking out her abused pack of cancer sticks. 'Here,' she said, placing the cigarette between my lips with her right hand and lighting it with the left. She lit one for herself too.

'I'm trying to quit,' I informed her for no apparent reason, enjoying the feeling of smoke traveling down my throat.

'How's *that* working out for you?' she mocked me. Her giggle followed me up the ladder to the roof.

No evidence was to be found.

Chapter Nineteen

Karouanos supermarket was a large, sprayed-white building with big red neon lights. On every window, the sign BUILDING FOR SALE OR RENT, gave off the desperation of the owners who were hit hard by the economic crisis that plagued Greece. Inside, the shelves were half full -or half empty, depending on how you view the metaphorical glass.

Two girls, dressed in black trousers and red shirts, worked the checkout counters. An obese man, in his fifties, was complaining for not finding his favorite brand of cereal.

'I don't drive and I'm not going to take the bus all the way to Carrefour,' he muttered on his way out.

'What's his problem, Stella?' The question came from a head that popped out from behind the shelves of the food aisle.

'Nothing, Mister Karouano. Just Mr. Gianni being Mr. Gianni!'

'Stella?'

She turned and stared at me. She studied me for a quick second and asked how she might help me.

'I am Captain Papacosta and this is Lieutenant Cara.' I pointed to Ioli, who was standing by the entrance, reading the shop's leaflet with the weekly offers.

'Yes?' she drawled the question, accompanying it with wide eyes.

'We are here regarding the death of Kate Spanou. If we could have a moment of your time, if you are not busy,' I said and looked around at the deserted store.

'Don't know how *I* can help you, but...' she lifted her hands up and shouted out to her boss that she would be going outside for a cigarette break. She got up and walked out, throwing looks at her co-worker who had already started texting friends that Stella had been taken away by the police. Nothing like good gossip to start the day in a small society.

We followed her fake purple nails and comfortable black flat shoes to the side of the building. It had shade and was out of sight. The red bricked wall reminded me of my high school in Astoria. Against such walls, bullies like Franklin Carter and his gang tortured skinny nerdy foreign little me on a daily basis. Until I punched him hard in the face and broke his nose, that is. Sent home, suspended for a week, yelled at by my mother, smacked by my father and frowned upon by my teacher, Miss Jenny. But it was worth it. I had earned myself the tag of being a hard-ass. A name I maintained all the way up to police academy.

Stella pulled her deep copper hair into a high ponytail and with trembling fingers, the thirty year old brought a cigarette to her lips. She offered us one, receiving a stern no from Ioli and a fake one from me.

'So, what have you heard?' The question came out with alluring smoke.

'What was the nature of your relationship with Mario Spanou, Mrs...?' Ioli asked.

More trembling. More smoke.

'Listen, I am a married woman and you know how islands are. I... I...'

'That is why it is best for you to answer our questions here than down at the station. You can just say, we are checking up on everyone who knew them. We already have a team going door to door. Whatever you say will be in confidence.'

'It's Mrs. Georgiou by the way, but call me Stella,' she forced a flat line smile. 'Mario and I were close. Intimate, if you know what I mean.'

I nodded my head to show that I did. Ioli smiled and gently touched Stella's shoulder. A woman on the verge of breaking down in tears. For the moment, we were both playing good cop.

'It just happened. We were both unhappy in our marriages, not that that's an excuse. He shopped here and was so kind and handsome. He made me feel special. And now, he's gone. I never knew Kate well. I had nothing against her. I feel bad that someone shot her, but I don't see why you are here.'

'We have to explore all leads...' I started to say.

'You think *I* shot her?'

'No one is saying that...'

'Since Mario died, I have only been here and at home. Anyway, why would I want her dead? Mario is dead, what would I have to gain from her death? And those poor little angels, left orphans!' She fell into Ioli's arms and wept. She had been brave enough to hold her tears for a lost lover, but now, overwhelmed with buried emotions that were surfacing fast and away from non-understanding eyes, especially her cheated-on husband's, she collapsed. Ioli had no sympathy for the adulteress. Always a firm believer that if you are unhappy, you leave and move on. She gradually pushed the woman away, holding her by the shoulders. She looked straight into Stella's watery red eyes.

'Maybe you blamed her for Mario. He did die during sex. She screwed him to death,' Ioli said, hoping anger would provide answers.

'Don't say that! He did not sleep with her anymore!'

'Not only with her, but we heard he was quite the ladies' man.'

'Shut it! You don't know shit! Mario loved me! And yes, if she killed him, I would have killed the bitch, but he died of a heart attack. My Mario had a weak heart! Now, if I am not under arrest, I have to get back to work. Haven't got all day to stand around and listen to your rude mouth!'

'You're free to go,' I said and watched the woman storm off while bringing to life one more cigarette.

'That went well,' Ioli smiled.

'You do have your way with women! Anyway, I doubt she did it.'

'What if Kate did kill her husband? Or what if someone killed them both? I think we need to dig up dear Mario and get that dinosaur doctor and his helper to perform an autopsy. If his wife or anyone killed him, it will be poison. A scorned woman's favorite murder weapon.'

'Especially knowing he had a weak ticker.'

Chapter Twenty

Days later, the autopsy results confirmed that poison brought Mario down. Large amounts of antifreeze were found in his blood stream. Kate had managed to feed it to him. A housewife can learn a lot from internet articles and YouTube videos.

Not that it mattered anyway, in terms of solving the case, that is. The very next day, after our talk with Stella at the supermarket, we had two more dead bodies on our hands.

After leaving the closing-down supermarket, we visited the one-foot-in-the-grave medical examiner and asked for an autopsy. I had already contacted our people in Athens to get the paperwork going and sent Constable Christina Dionysiou to Mario's mother. The widow, dressed in black, signed the exhumation papers.

'Never trusted that bitch,' she hissed; her face shrivelled up by a cocktail of pain and hate. For a dead Greek, Kate Spanou got cursed a lot in the afterlife. No sugar-coated tales that normally come after death.

Our next meeting brought tears to our eyes. We parked the patrol car, provided by the local police department, outside of Kate's mother's house. A well-preserved one floor bungalow built in the sixties. The wooden fence was freshly painted and the pathway from the gate to the front door had been renovated with shiny looking beige bricks. Rose bushes welcomed us with that wild winter scent of theirs. The aluminium door flew open before we reached the two steps at the end of the beige brick road.

A petite woman in her late sixties, dressed from head to toe in pitch black clothing, with silver hair falling around her elfin face, waited for us to approach.

'Good evening, ma'am. I am Captain Papacosta and this is Lieutenant Ioli Cara. We are here...'

'What's good about it?'

'Our sincere condolences for your loss...' Ioli started to say.

'Come in. Come in.' She waved her wrinkly hands with difficulty, inviting us in.

The living room spread before us a ghost of its once spotless glory. A cloak of house dust covered the cherry wooden furniture and the countless photo frames. Small or large, silver or plastic. All dusty. Opposite the frames, a TV was tuned to a cartoon network and two girls sat in silence on the terracotta sofa. Kate's mother sat between them and switched off the TV. Neither girl retaliated. She gestured for us to sit on the two armchairs opposite her, next to the TV set.

'Hello girls,' Ioli said with a sincere smile. Neither replied. The youngest, aged five stared at us, a spitting image of her mother, while the oldest, aged seven, was a mixture of both her parents. The oldest had huge eyes and with the sadness surrounding her, she reminded me of a Keane painting.

'Girls, go up to your room and play... Quietly.'

Both stood up and like robots executed their grand-mother's request. Two tragic orphan figures made their way up the stairs. A door closing creaked from the floor above.

'Can I offer you anything to drink?' Greek hospitality prevailed under any circumstances.

'Thank you, Mrs. Moutsina. We are fine. We just need to ask you a few questions, if you are up for it.'

'Better now, than after. My daughter is never coming back and I have to be strong for those two little girls.'

We went through the typical set of questions, noting down whereabouts, close friends and words spoken.

'Thank you for all your help, Mrs. Moutsina,' Ioli said and we both stood up, closing our notepads.

She looked up at us, unsatisfied with the end of the interview.

'Have you looked into Mario's girlfriends?' She took one look at our faces. 'What? You thought I did not know? Everyone knew.'

'Did your daughter know?' Ioli asked.

'Of course she did! She just chose not to pay attention. She saw only the good in him. Had a real Cinderella complex with him, she used to joke. Never marry a man that handsome. Not even if you're a top model. I told her; a man is only as faithful as his options. I saw the danger in a union of Mario with my Katerina, but she was too foolish to see it. I mean, even water knows to jump off the griddle when it's hot. But Kate stayed and now she's gone.' Her throat closed and she said no more. She looked up to an icon of the Holy Mary, high above the fireplace, and tears ran down the deep trenches of her wan face.

I pulled some inner courage together and managed to form the question.

'Knowing your daughter, do you believe she would be capable of hurting Mario?'

'Never! She loved him too much,' she answered without turning.

We left her in her pain. A pain well-wishers say goes away with time, but that is just a lie. A lie we tell because we don't know what else to say. My daughter was murdered, eight years old. Four years have passed since then and the pain is still there, still real. A hole in my very existence, my soul in grief. I am a broken man without fear of dying. A man avoiding any kind of human attachment. No, pain does not go away.

We drove in silence. Santorini's capital, Thira was the cleanest town I had ever seen. Good, clean roads, trees and bushes trimmed and planted according to plan, houses and shops freshly painted and the few people that were brave enough to face the evening's cold breath, had a friendly Greek island smile decorating their faces. Every now and then a gap between houses offered the most spectacular view. The sea, painted orange as the winter sun approached it, calmly met the sky above.

Santorini offers the best sunset on the planet.

Ioli said that all you have to do is google 'Santorini Sunset' and fall in love.

Wild winds howled outside, warning people to stay inside. Freezing air roamed the narrow roads and hurried our pace into the local police station. The two constables had returned from going door-to-door and had prepared four steaming hot chocolates, each with two floating marsh-mallows.

We found out many things in the next half an hour.

Constable Christina made one hell of an amazing hot choco.

Constable Hercules had a real name. Costas Loukaki. His grandfather was from Crete. That alone earned a ten minute conversation between Hercules and Ioli. Places, names, stories were all fished out of memory and laid on the table.

Nefeles Suites was the name of the hotel we were going to stay in.

'I know it sounds fancy and all, but it is a three star. And for a three star it offers the best rooms and views on the island,' Christina said. The unwritten police budget rule was not to stay in four or five star hotels. Three —and even lower- was more appropriate.

We also found out that snow could fall on even such a tropical island. Pure white flakes flew outside, swirling around careless and free. Small Greek flakes though, not enough to pile up, not like snow in Astoria, New York, where little Costa made his first snowman and caught a cold making his first snow angel. Yes, not that kind of snow, for sure.

Unfortunately, we found out that by reading through reports formed by the door-to-door day trip, you learn a lot of pointless gossip, write down quite a few times *I saw nothing, I wasn't home, I can't help you* and you wonder how a gunshot went unnoticed on a Monday morning.

Costa Loukaki A.K.A. Hercules, programmed our patrol car's GPS and proudly announced that we would find our hotel without problems.

'Only problem is there's no parking. It is on the edge of the cliff, like most of our hotels. You park three minutes away,' Christina popped his bubble.

Ioli made her *well-what-to-do* gesture and I assured them

that we would be fine. Fine was not how things went down. Slipping down and landing hard on my ass was not fine. Ioli stepping in a deep, frozen, blood-stopping puddle was not fine. By the time we reached the hotel, we looked like something that even the cat would not drag in.

'Welcome to Nefeles,' the kind brunette said with a warm, inviting smile and eyes full of kindness. A rare sight in Athens. The norm on the islands.

We introduced ourselves and with cold water invading through our clothes we followed the cheerful receptionist into areas with strong central heating. The place had a homey feeling to it with wooden furniture and paintings in earthy tones. Large vases hosted long fake flowers and tall bamboo sticks, while a narrow river of pool water ran beside us. I gazed around, happy by the choice of hotel, while Ioli looked worried about our dirty shoe marks that decorated the once clean and polished floor tiles.

The chatty receptionist spoke all the way to our rooms' doors.

'Your rooms are cozy, open plan style bedrooms with sitting areas and of course panoramic views of the volcano! The bathroom is marble lined with an amazing bathtub. You have a private balcony with stunning views. The heating is on. Anything you need to make a cup of tea or coffee is available, and we have satellite TV. Not just central European crap, we have movie channels, sports channels, you name it, discovery channel, animal planet. You won't believe the things I have learnt from flicking through them. Not so busy here in the winter! Anyway, anything else you may need just dial 0 on the phone and I will be at your service. Here are your keys. 201 for the gentleman and 202 for the lady. Enjoy your stay!' And off she went, wishing good evening to a senior couple, probably on their fourth honeymoon following their wedding vow renewal after fifty years of the ball and chain.

'Thank God, she's gone. If she named one more damn channel, my headache was ready to swing into full migraine,' Ioli said, holding the upper part of her nose and squinting her eyes.

'And that face helps?'

'With all due respect, screw you, Captain,' she laughed out loud. 'Okay, go shower, change and I'll come over with our food options.'

I did not argue. My tummy was making its crocodile noises and I knew Ioli would go past migraine and into bitch mode if she did not feed soon.

Twenty five minutes later, room service A.K.A. chatty receptionist found us both shiny and refreshed in the sitting area A.K.A. sofa with coffee table. Ioli had ordered pork chops with oregano and onions, golden, Cypriot, oven potatoes and a Greek salad with fresh and juicy-looking tomatoes and cucumbers. Feta cheese covered the top of the salad and olive oil painted it green. I looked at the two ice-cold Mythos beers and smiled.

'You remembered my beer?'

'Let's dig in.' Her excitement was wrapped around every word she said.

I let her enjoy her meal, before attempting to ask what had been on my mind, days in and days out.

'You feeling okay...being back?'

'Want a simple yes?'

'Not really.'

'Yeah, it sucked that I got shot and it hurt like a motherfucker, but three months of therapy brought my body back to shape.'

'And your mind?'

'Mama helped with that. Being home felt good but... with the risk of sounding like some psycho freak, I missed work, murders and all.'

'Your mama is one great lady.'

'Yes, she is. Though we argued every Sunday when she tried to wake me up for church.'

'Not religious, Ioli?'

Her eyes opened wide, she flashed me her pearly white teeth and took a sip from her beer. 'You know, it's a weird topic for me. I mean, like all Greeks, my parents woke me every Sunday and took me to church. School took us, grandmothers took us. We went on all the major holidays and our houses are filled with icons. And, there's me, doubting everything. Sitting there, unable to switch my thoughts off.'

'Doubting what exactly?'

'Not God himself, but all this Saint this, and do this, and pray like this, and dress like this, eat this and not that... I mean, what the fuck does food have to do with your soul? My parents ate a huge bowl of delicious black-eyed beans with Greek pumpkin and tuna and olive oil and bread, and my aunt brought cake made of some sort of non-dairy fake chocolate. That is not fasting. I mean, why is it a sin to eat a tiny burger? The amount is smaller.' She paused. 'I sound silly, don't I?'

'No, no. I get where you're coming from. I had the same upbringing. I never thought about doubts until Gaby died. What God kills children, right? Then, I accepted that God does not interfere with us, free will and all, and I just live each day, working, doing good to society and when death comes, maybe answers will appear.'

'Or maybe we will rot into nothingness...'

'Does death scare you?'

'Not death itself. The idea that everything we do is in vain, if there is nothing to follow.'

'To life after death,' I raised my voice and my beer. Her beer met mine and with an 'ygeia mas' and a 'kalinyxta', we went our separate ways.

I stripped down to my black boxers and fell like a log on top of the bed. The central heating was enough for my thick skin. Ioli went to her room, brushed her teeth, let her hair loose, took off her minimal make-up, washed and scrubbed her face, undressed, wore her light-blue pyjamas with the cute penguins printed down the side, dived under the warm bed covers and picked up her Kindle Fire from the 1940's bedside table. She felt happy; her favorite writer, Lena Manta, had added a mystery book to her portfolio.

'The five keys...' she read to herself. Her police mind pretty much figured out the culprit early on, but she enjoyed being transferred to her *reading land*. Page 102 was hard to read. Not due to the subject matter though. Falling eyelids made it hard. She switched off the light and her Kindle, assumed her sleeping position and whispered, 'goodnight, God. Keep mama and papa safe. Amen.'

The next thing that we heard was the banging on our doors. Hercules banged away on mine, while Christina knocked on Ioli's door.

'One minute,' I managed to say. Two words more than I usually manage at six in the morning. Ioli uttered more words than me. Most were a repetition of the f-word or combinations of the f-word with others. The girl did have a good imagination when it came to her profanity vocabulary. My ears managed to electrify my mind's inner circuit and I formed the words coming out of Hercules's mouth into a sentence.

Stella had hanged herself.

Her husband noticed her missing from their bed, opened their bedroom door and found her swinging above the stairs. He ran to his lifeless wife, crying, shouting, holding her up. His love was gone. She hung colder than the night. The small note in her hand, gave way to rage. Enough fury to strangle his pain.

FOR MARIO... SEE YOU SOON.

Tears now fell for an entirely different reason. He sat down on the last step, shaking, hitting the railing with his fists. Then he sat in silence. Blank mind. When he felt ready, he called it in.

Chapter Twenty-One

NEW YORK

Mister Sebastianos, Sebastian to all his friends, woke up and praised the Lord for another day. He praised Him even more, when a whiff of bacon and eggs came out of the kitchen and into the room. After peeing for the seventh time in the last ten hours, he trudged down the corridor, stopping at Jesus' icon that hung between family photos. He kissed the icon and thought of the good life he had lived. Through the bad, good always managed to prevail. He did not always agree with the Lord for sending the bad, but he felt thankful for the good.

His wife, Maria, was busy over a hot pan. Both were in their late seventies and still very much in love. He hugged her from behind and laid a gentle, tender kiss on her neck. They both enjoyed breakfast together, now they had retired. They ate what they wanted, for as long as they wanted. No train to catch, no 'I'm late for work', no telling the kids to hurry up. Even on Sundays -church day- they would have breakfast after church as to enjoy it at their own pace.

'Have we got plans?' Sebastian asked, teeth still grinding a juicy piece of back bacon.

Maria smiled. 'You mean, have I got chores for you? No, you are free!'

His weird soft laughter widened her smile further along her round face.

'Great. I'm going down to the park to play chess with the boys.'

'In this weather?'

'First day without rain. We said on the first day it stops raining, whoever is still alive, to gather in the park for a chess tournament!' Now, it was her turn to laugh.

'Well, I hope all your friends are still alive.'

That was his plan for the day. Chess tournament. Until lunch, that was. Maria promised to make his favorite. Moussaka, salad and his collection of much-needed pills.

With his brown flat cap on and his jacket's collar pulled up all Dracula style, as he referred to it, he exited onto Ditmar's Boulevard. He walked close to the wall of the red bricked apartment blocks to keep out of the cold wind's path. He shot straight to the Agnanti Greek Tavern, on the corner of 19th street. In old man's time, he was late, and the boys had already drunk their first morning coffee and were across the street, by one of the park's many entrances.

'Sebastian's here, too!' John declared with a loud voice that made him cough and the gang to laugh.

'Keep it down. You don't wanna give yourself another heart attack!' Pier joked.

Sebastian rushed to cross over. A fine day for chess, but definitely not a fine day for Abigail Moore. Everything that could delay her had happened and now she sped down the road, coffee in one hand, her morning cigarette in the other. Her eye caught a glimpse of a shadowy figure in front of her Ford Explorer SUV. She dropped her coffee in an attempt to turn the wheel and stepped down on the brakes. The icy road did her no favors. She hit Sebastian hard and threw him high into the air. Gravity pulled him back down to earth and his head hit the sidewalk. Blood ebbed out of his open skull.

Back home, Maria whistled away, busy with her moussaka preparations when the phone rang. John coughed to clear his throat. His words came from his weak heart.

'Maria, there's been an accident. Sebastian was hit by a car. The ambulance picked him up. I am sending my daughter to pick you up. Be strong, Maria. Sebastian is a fighter.'

Maria fell to the floor. Her heart pounded so loud, she thought it would jump out of her chest. She closed her eyes, prayed to the Theotokos Mary and gathered enough courage to pull herself up.

Chapter Twenty-Two

Jacob Hatzinikolaou, sat silent and morose on a white, plastic patio chair. He seemed unable to speak or face the house. He wore only his boxers and a thin Olympiakos T-shirt. It was just a few degrees above zero, but the cold did not seem to bother him. Constable Christina approached him and covered him in one of those ugly, itchy, grey police blankets. He did not pay any attention to her. The paramedics stood by the door. They had checked Stella for vital signs and waited for the police to arrive and give the okay for the body's removal.

Ioli entered first and I followed close behind. The body had stopped swinging. The first sunrays were sneaking in from behind charcoal clouds and thin curtains, shedding light upon the frigid corpse. Stella had used thick rope, borrowed from her husband's shed. Jacob was quite the handyman and had all 'kinds of crap' as she often referred to his stuff. She had tied the rope around the staircase chandelier and jumped from the top step, snapping her neck in a matter of seconds. Her yellow Snoopy pyjamas and her pink toenails were in full contrast to the macabre scene.

Ioli stretched her latex gloves and picked up the ball of paper beneath the dead woman. She unfolded it carefully.

'For Mario, see you soon,' she read.

'That would explain the husband's state.'

'Love should be announced as the number one cause of death, if you ask me,' Ioli said and continued to examine the body. I stood beside her, scanning the body.

'Suicide?'

'Looks like it,' I replied, checking her pyjama pockets. Both empty.

'Wife finds out about affair, wife poisons husband? Husband's mistress shoots wife and then throws herself to death?' I was not sure if Ioli was talking to me or mumbling to herself, searching for reason.

'Wouldn't be the first time. A timeless tale on which countless books, movies and series are based on.'

Outside Constable Christina managed to get Jacob's statement. Not that he had much to say. With my permission, she let the paramedics take him to the hospital. His parents and his sisters were notified for support. The old relic of a doctor arrived too, announced that Stella had died two hours ago and ordered the men with him to bring the body to the ambulance. He was in a rush to get out of the cold. Unusual for someone born during the last ice-age.

I loosened the rope.

'Ever attained fingerprints from a rope?' Ioli asked, knowing it was hopeless. That is when it hit her. I saw it, in her eyes.

'She smoked with her left hand. Call Christina to ask her husband if she was left handed.'

Ioli waited eagerly as I spoke. I lowered my phone. Stella was indeed left handed.

'Does this look like a knot tied by a left-handed person?'

'Well, I'll be damned...'

Chapter Twenty-Three

After two hours of collecting evidence from the murder scene, we were back at the police station, waiting for Christina to bring in Jacob for questioning. Her apple-shaped body and hazelnut long wavy hair were soon visible through the glass door. Jacob walked in first as she held the door for him. He was dressed this time. He wore a pair of jeans and a black, leather jacket, zipped all the way to the top. His bloodshot eyes were dry of tears. Christina introduced us and escorted him to interrogation room one. He zombie-walked behind her. We followed and sat down opposite him. Christina excused herself and off she went to prepare coffees for all.

'We are so sorry for your loss, Mr. Hatzinikolaou, and we are sorry to have to bring you in just hours after your wife's death, but it's important that your memory is fresh.'

He looked at me emotionless as I spoke. With a slight nod, he seemed to agree with what I said.

'Did you hear anything last night, Mr. Hatzinikolaou?'

'Please call me Jacob. That runway of a surname will leave you breathless,' he joked, yet remained in the same pitiful state. We smiled and let him continue in his own time. 'I sleep heavy. I mean, real heavy. Always had trouble with school attendance and in the army? Don't ask. Anyway, it must have been around six o'clock when I turned and realized I was alone in bed. I got up, peed and called out for Stella. She did not answer, so I went to find her and... There she was. Killed herself. For another man.' The last three words came out with so much anger. Fury burned in his eyes. 'Do you know how long she had been seeing him?' he clenched his fists and asked.

'I'm sorry, but no.'

'I fucking went fishing with the guy. Saw him in the pub. That mother...' He slammed down his clenched fists on the table. 'Sorry,' he rushed to add.

'Jacob, I won't even pretend to understand what you are going through at the moment, but you need to relax and think hard if you heard or saw anything. Anything suspicious, maybe? Out of the ordinary?'

He looked puzzled. 'No... But... Erm... why are you asking? Was someone with her?'

'What size shoe do you wear, Jacob?' Ioli asked.

'Forty-two...' He looked even more puzzled.

'There were footprints on your carpet. Size forty-five. Know anyone with a size forty-five shoe?'

'Wait, she had help?'

'Or maybe she had *too* much help? Was the note in her handwriting?'

Christina pushed open the door with her body and with a faint smile, she left the coffees, a plate filled with vanilla cream biscuits and without saying a word, she exited the room.

'Can I see the note again? I didn't pay much attention to it the first time.'

'Sure.' Ioli placed the nylon evidence bag containing the note before him. Jacob studied it for a second and announced that it was indeed Stella's handwriting. I showed him a photograph of the rope. He recognized it as his own from his shed.

'Do you think she was... murdered?'

'We don't know, Jacob, but we have to examine every angle. Can you think of anyone who would want to hurt her? Any threats made?'

He shook his head. We drank coffee and listened to his stories about how loved his Stella was. He was a man in torment. But, did he hurt enough to kill her?

'For me, if we can prove that knew about the affair, he is the main suspect,' Ioli said, after Jacob had left. 'He truly loved her!'

Ioli spent the rest of the day, labelling fingerprints lifted from the house and faxing them to HQ. She got in touch with the medical examiner, who confirmed death by spinal rupture. No other bruising than that caused by the rope. She had no defensive wounds. Everything pointed to a clear case of suicide.

Just as the evening rolled in and Ioli began to doubt her theory, I called.

Constable Christina and I were out making door-to-door enquiries in the freezing cold. At least, it did not rain or snow. By the time we reached the last house on the street, I was looking more and more like Rudolf and his famous nose. So far, no-one had seen anything. Every single person had been asleep around the time of death. Some houses were completely empty; overflowing post boxes giving away that the owners only stayed here during the lively summer months, which here in Greece are April, May, June, July, August *and* September. For the islands, you could add October, too.

No early birds on Mitropoleos Street. A quiet street with few houses, a closed-for-the-winter cafe, a couple of shops and one vacant plot overgrowing with January weeds. The last house, opposite the empty plot, looked the oldest of the lot. It begged for a fresh splash of paint. In the front garden plants that survived the drought fought hard to come back to life on winter's rain. The wooden steps leading to the main door looked unsafe and an old black Ford Capri from the 70's stood dead in the open door garage. It looked as if it had not been driven in the last ten years; rust and dust had completely covered it and some smart-ass had fingered-written *I wish my wife was this dirty* on it.

I knocked, softer than usual. The door looked ready to say goodbye to this world. The windows were open, the worn-in curtains flying out into the wind. Old sixties hits were playing inside. I knocked again.

'I'm coming, I'm coming. Hold your horses! I heard you the first time!' a croaky manly voice came from inside. The door was pulled back and a strong smell of cigars hit us.

'Come in, come in and wipe your feet,' the short man ordered in the same manner he told off kids and grandkids, whenever they remembered he was still alive and visited him.

He wobbled from side to side, wooden walking stick in one hand, cigar in the other.

'Tea? Coffee?'

'Sir, I am Captain...'

'Yeah, yeah, you're the cops. I figured that much out. You've been going door-to-door for the last few hours. Tea or coffee? You look like a coffee guy.'

My face showed my agreement.

'And you, beautiful?' he asked Christina, in a tender manner and not in that dirty, old man's manner.

'Tea would be fine, thank you.'

'I'll make you a mint tea. My wife used to love a strong mint tea this time of day.' And with that, he trotted off to the kitchen. We sat down on the brown sofa and waited. It was our last house and we were tired. We could spare ten minutes and enjoy a hot cup with a lonely old man.

Soon, introductions were made and we were enjoying our beverage with Mr. Papadopoulos. He insisted we called him Billy. Made him feel young, he admitted with a mischievous grin.

'Sorry bout the mess. I live alone. Lost my Eleni two years now. Kids all live in Athens.'

'This is an amazing cup of tea.'

'Always use fresh mint. Everyone uses dry mint for some reason. Too lazy to go buy fresh, I guess. So, you are here for that Stella woman?'

'Yes. We were wondering if you may have seen something suspicious even though your house is quite far from hers.'

'Yes, everyone wants a view. That is why I bought this land cheap, even back then and why the opposite plot is empty. Too expensive that one. Everyone wants to see the sunset. My shades are so rusty, the sun is always orange to me!' He laughed out loud. We joined him until his laughter was cut off by his cough.

'Stupid old age! Can't even laugh anymore! Anyway, I watch CSI, Law and Order, Dexter, Castle, Sherlock, you name it. After Mrs. Georgiou next door said the police were going around asking about the hanging, I noted down all the cars that I remember being on the street at half past five when I woke up.' He pulled out a once-blank, piece of paper. He had my full attention.

'Out of the twelve cars, eleven belong to people living on the street. One doesn't. And it was parked across from my house. I've cracked the case, right?' He was beaming with self-satisfaction.

'I believe you have! What car was it?'

He glowed in victory even more. I expected his bald head to start giving off light. 'It was a 2004 white Fiat Strada. And before you go searching your database for owners, I can do you one better. It had a logo on the side. YourWoodWorker.Gr.'

'That's in Kamari, by the airport,' Christina said. 'I've met the owner. A John something. He did some work on my parent's house a couple of years back.'

We thanked Billy for his services. He told us to visit again.

Menacing clouds threw their first warning shots. I called Ioli with the news. By the time we parked outside the station to pick her up, it was really pissing it down.

Christina jumped out of the patrol car and Ioli came running out of the building, *Beautiful people* covered her silky black hair that she had pulled back in a bun. Christina vanished through the open door, glad to be back close to central heating. The cold on the islands penetrated your skin and chilled your bones. Something about the sea air, I guess. In New York, if you dressed warm enough, you could tolerate the cold easy. Here, you could wear all your clothes and still feel the ice settling on your bones.

The GPS lady with her fine math skills, calculated the distance to 8.7 KM and twelve minutes as our estimated time of arrival. The country road was not bad, considering that with all the cuts due to the country's financial crisis, no maintenance occurred anymore. The wipers were working at full speed and the thunder in the sky, drowned out the car's radio. Not that we were listening to it. I brought Ioli up to date with our Mr. Billy visit.

In seventeen minutes (I'm looking at *you*, GPS lady), we were outside a lonely bricked warehouse with a tin roof. The rain fell upon it hard, its drum-like music echoing through the surrounding fields by the country road from the airport to the village of Kamari. We drove up to the building and in haste found ourselves under the wooden pergola that covered the entrance. The aluminium door below the sign YourWoodWorker.Gr was open. The wind banging it, yet never closing it. Inside, it was quiet like a grave. Ioli walked in, pistol secure between both her hands. I pulled out my gun and stood by the open door.

'Hello?' No answer.

'John?'

Again, no reply. Just the wind howling through gaps in the bricked wall. We both stood in the vast, open space. A damp and draughty place. Planks of wood and worktables filled the space.

'Police! Is anyone here?' Ioli called out, her gun moving around, covering the ground.

'Looks clear,' I said, and that was when we heard a faint, screeching sound. The rain was dying down and quiet spread across the valley. The sound echoed clearer this time. It came from the office in the rear end of the warehouse. With guns held straight ahead, we approached.

Suddenly, a noise from below. A huge rat ran beside Ioli's left foot. She whispered a curse that found its way out from behind gritted teeth.

The noise now clear and familiar. It reminded me of my daughter playing on our neighborhood swings. I turned the knob and pushed open the door, jumping in the room with my gun ready to threaten. I froze at the sight of the hanging naked body. Ioli gasped for air and her eyes widened in shock.

Before us, a man was suspended by his arms and feet from the ceiling, face down. Thick metal wire tied to a hook on the ceiling held his wrists together. Same with his ankles. Blood dripped from his head, mouth and nose, forming a pool of blood beneath him. A second, smaller pool formed by drops of blood dripping from his dangling genitals. Ioli walked around.

'What the...?' Her hand covered her mouth in disgust. His anus was held open by a weird ring, a green sex toy. He was badly bruised, showing signs of severe rape.

I placed two fingers on his neck's main artery. He was dead, yet the body, even in this cold, was still quite warm. He died during the last two hours.

'Costa, how is this all connected?' she asked, panic gently covering each word.

'Either this guy was killed by the same murderer who killed Stella or this guy killed Stella and was killed by another?' The repetition of the word killed, gave away my confusion. Too many puzzle pieces and no box cover to look at.

As I called Christina and the medical examiner, Ioli searched around the building. No one was to be seen. She came back, hunting rifle in her latex-covered hand.

'Think I found Kate's murder weapon...'

'Lift it for prints,' I said and called the chief to let him know about the unexpected turn our case had just taken. I also requested all evidence and DNA to be sent to the top of the list.

Half an hour later, Hercules and the coroner's apprentice, whose name I still don't know, lowered down the body.

His back housed a plethora of tattoos. A cross, head shots of Saint John and Saint Mina, and a couple of passages from the Bible.

FOR GOD SO LOVED THE WORLD, THAT HE GAVE HIS ONE AND ONLY SON, THAT WHOEVER BELIEVES IN HIM SHALL NOT PERISH BUT HAVE ETERNAL LIFE - JOHN 3:16

'For all have sinned and fall short of the glory of God,' Ioli read the other.

What a way to die. Not that there is a good way. I don't feel like dying old, senile and with shitty diapers on, in some nursing home or worse in some smelly hospital with bitchy nurses that wait for you to die cause they need the bed for the next old, senile fart with diapers on. No. Sir. There is not a good way to go.

Loud ground shaking thunder killed my flow of thoughts. The body of John Mina was bagged and rolled out of his workplace. Bruise-colored clouds covered the little blue left in the sky and swallowed the orange ball burning behind them, ready to dip into the horizon and call it a night. The paramedics were having a difficult time wheeling him through the muddy pathway. The strong rain gathered momentum and a wrong step, in a wrong puddle, brought the first paramedic to her knees. Her colleague was busy pushing the stretcher, rushing to leave the rainy outdoors. He hit her hard with the stretcher on her forehead opening up a nice blood-producing, stitches-needing scar, that would be the talk of the week at the local hospital. The body bag fell to the left and rolled in the mud.

No, Ma'am. There is not a good way to go.

John was a simple man and so was his workplace.

He only had what he needed, mostly tools. Receipts and orders filled his office drawers. No family photographs, no holiday souvenirs, no needless junk. A practical man. On his desk, an outdated computer -the ones where the screen is triple the size of the modem, a brown, vintage, rotary dial telephone and a black hardcover Bible.

His home did not differ.

He lived alone in a one bedroom apartment in the nearby village of Kamari. Never married, never fathered offspring. A forty year old that kept to himself, never socializing with the neighbors. He had a bed to sleep on, a table to eat on, an oven to cook in and a fridge to keep the milk cold. No sign of a TV or a couch.

The night sky filled with a glowing slice of moon and millions of flickering white dots, and signalled the end of a rainy day. A single lonely cloud shipped through the stars. It was a peaceful ride back to our hotel. Our case puzzled us both. Both of us needed reason to prevail.

Ioli spoke first. 'He kept to himself, no friends, no family... But he was religious. The tattoos, the Bible, the icons above his bed.'

'Pay his local church a visit in the morning?'

'No.'

'No?'

She couldn't help but smile.

'Keep your eyes on the road, please. His last name was Mina, he had Saint Mina tattooed on his back...'

'Saint Mina church in Thira.'

'And that's possibly where we'll find our connection. It is the church nearest to Kate and Stella. They both went to church on Sundays.'

'The local priest could help us. I doubt he'll be awake at this time of night.'

'First thing in the morning...'

She did not complete her thought. My ringtone bounced around the car.

'Annoying grandpa ringtone,' Ioli commented *once again*. I ignored her remark *once again*. It was turning into a thing. Into one of those annoying routine lines we humans tend to say. A Pavlovian response to a sound, smell, picture, movement.

Unknown US number.

'Hello?'

'Costa? Costa, my boy,' was all my mother, Maria, managed to say without crying. The rest came with tears and sobbing.

'Mama? You okay? What's wrong?'

'It's your father, Costa.' My heart skipped a beat. The better part of my brain used instinct and pulled over, parking the car on the muddy side of the road, killing fresh grass as the vehicle came to a full stop. I had never heard this tone of voice with her. I was expecting her next words to be *your father is dead*.

'Costa, can you hear me?'

'Yes, mama!' My voice rocketed to the high eighties of the dB scale. Ioli jumped in her seat. She laid her hand gently on my shoulder. Her smile letting me know that she was there for me.

'He's been hit by a car...'

'A car? How? How's dad?'

'On his way to the park. He just got out of surgery...'

'And now you call?' I regretted yelling at her immediately.

'I was in shock. I stood outside the door, going up and down like crazy!'

'I know, Mama. Sorry. Is dad okay now?'

'They don't know. This young blond doctor said she did all she could, but he is old and things don't repair like when we are young. He hasn't woken up, Costa! He might not...'

The last words struggled to come out her mouth. She could not say any more.

'Call Auntie Tonia. Don't be alone.'

'I will. I will. All his friends are here, too. When can you get here?'

'Me? Mama, I can't leave...'

'Costa, he's your father! He is dying and you...' The same angry voice I heard only once before. I was fourteen when the police came round our house. They were doing rounds asking all the neighborhood boys if we knew anything about Panayiota Karaoli's rape. She was fifteen at the time. She was returning home, late at night, and walked through the park where all the block's teens hang out. She was attacked from behind, blindfolded and pulled into the trees. Her hands were tied together and her legs spread apart. She felt scissors cut off her jean shorts, her Disney sweatshirt and her sports bra. She could not recall how many had their way with her as they took turns raping her. They left her there, bruised, bloody and scared. The following morning, the news spread like wildfire in our small, Greek community. Everyone was a suspect. Especially, teenage boys to whom the park served as a second home. The cops were sure one of us would know something. I had -without mama's permission- taken the metro with my mate Jimmy. We went to that Led Zeppelin concert we were not allowed to go to. The two cops towering me, asking me about my whereabouts the previous night were less scary than my mother. As I chewed on my words, making silly, unprepared excuses, she snapped!

'Now, listen here young man. You better start talking the truth right now or I swear to God and all the Saints that I will break you!' She was so worried that her good Christian boy had something to do with the rape that upon hearing I was at the concert, she fell into my arms and hugged me. Then she slapped me twice on my head. One for lying to the police and one for going to the concert. A third slap came as a warning not to do it again. Now, after all these years, the same angry tone was used.

'Mama, I am in the middle of a case. A murder case. I have four dead bodies...'

'Soon you will have a fifth.'

'Mama, don't be bitter. I'm in Santorini. A killer is on the loose. Dad is alive, and he is a fighter. I'll fly out as soon as the case is over.'

'I need you. But you stay there with your bodies. Save lives.'

'Mama...' The crackling noise came through sounding the slamming of the hospital phone's handset. She was pissed off, and she had every right to be. I was her only son. She needed me there. Hopefully, my sister Jo who I bet she called straight after me, would fly out of Seattle immediately. Hopefully, Aunt Tonia who lived round the corner would be there in five. Mama always hated being alone. Especially in times like these. My father had always stood by her, through every wedding vow. Through sickness and all that.

'Costa, is your father okay?' Ioli quietly asked.

'A car hit him... He hasn't woken up yet.'

'My God...' Her breath quickened its pace.

'God! It's times like these I wonder what kind of sick games he likes to play. We just saw a religious man hanging naked, brutally raped and killed. God. He took my daughter, he may take my father, somebody else's loved one is dying as we speak. All ages, all races, all kinds of people. Good, bad. All in the same pot. All contestants in the

GuessWhoDiesNextAndVoteHow, heaven's favorite TV show!'

'Get out. I'm driving.' She exited the car and walked around. In a furious zombie like state, I did the same. 'Let's get you back to the hotel big guy.'

She never questioned my decision to stay. She was a cop and, like me, this mess was her life. We caught killers. That's what we did. Everything else came second as horrible as that may sound to normal folk. She walked me to my door and asked if there was anything she could do for me.

'No, I'm fine. You go eat and get some shut eye. Seven o'clock sharp we'll meet for breakfast and head over to the church.' I forced a smile. I closed the door before she could see the first tear fall. With watery eyes, I found my cancer sticks and exited to the balcony. The stunning night view insignificant to me. I chained smoked four cigarettes before invading the mini bar. Mr. Walker and Mr. Daniels went down my throat before a fifth cigarette was lit. Same number of cigarettes that I smoked all of last year. I felt like a spoiled angry teen taking it out on my body. I felt stupid. And with that last thought, I undressed down to my boxers and fell on top of the soft bed.

Chapter Twenty-Four

DR. ARIADNE METAXA'S OFFICE

'It's good that you cried,' she said, widening her smile, glad her closed-book patient had finally opened up to her. Her lissome figure approached me and filled my glass up with expensive mineral water.

Normally, I would not be discussing police cases with a civilian, but Ariadne was kind of part of the force and shrinks had that whole I-can't-tell-shit-to-no-one confidentiality oath. 'I call tears soul catharsis. Were your tears just for your father?'

I shrugged. 'I don't know. Yeah. I wasn't thinking of anything else.' *Please do not make this about my daughter.*

'How did you feel when Ioli showed her support?'

I frowned. 'Good. It's always good to feel that you have someone there for you.' The sentence came out in the form of a question.

'I am not implying anything, Captain. I know your relationship is purely platonic. It's just that I know you have a hard time letting people get close.'

I laughed. Ariadne Metaxa, for the first time, looked

puzzled. She uncrossed her beautiful legs and crossed them the other way. In a modest way that is. No Basic Instinct style flash.

'Did I say something amusing, Costa?'

'No, no,' I quickly replied, my laughter dying down. 'You're right, once again. I don't let anyone in and Ioli is the first person I let get close to me since... since then.' *Then*. Murder. Divorce. Escape from New York. *Then*.

'I laughed at the word platonic,' I continued. 'My ADD mind played a scene from days past.'

'Tell me about it,' she said, leaning back into her chair. Her eyes studied me and her fingers began fidgeting with her well-sharpened rubber top pencil.

'I had this friend in high school. Melissa. Terrific girl. We talked a lot and went to the movies a couple of times. Purely platonic as you said. Well, one day as we were on the roof smoking -out of adults' sight- my mate Jimmy turned and asked if I had... *slept* with her yet.' Not the word he used, but I have never been a fan of the f-word. Unlike everyone I have ever met, here in Greece. 'I told him we were just friends. I still remember the shock on his face.' I did my best to mimic Jimmy's deep voice. 'Friends? You freaking serious? Sweet pussy like that! If a man needs a friend, he gets a dog!'

Ariadne's laugh was always the same. It was more of a giggle, a little girl's giggle. She knew that. That is why her laughter lasted exactly two seconds. A two second spontaneous giggle, abruptly shot down by her embarrassment. A light rose colored the skin on her high cheekbones. She exhaled and the color vanished. She became her professional self again.

'Maybe you should get a dog?'

'In my tiny apartment, with my hours? I had a hard

time feeding that stupid goldfish the woman next door gave me to babysit for a week. Do you have a dog?'

'No, unfortunately, I am a cat lady. And being unmarried with four cats screams spinster from a mile away.' Too personal; it lasted just a second and she moved on. 'So, four dead bodies, what happened next?'

'The lab results came in and boy, did we have a mystery on our hands! But, first we paid the local priest a visit.'

Chapter Twenty-Five

Agios Minas Church, like most churches in Thira, hung on the edge of the caldera, reachable only by foot. Narrow stone pathways lead to and pass by it, forcing drivers to abandon their cars a mile away. This was fine for the flocks of tourists in the summer; the church was probably the most photographed church on the island. But now, during winter, it was anything but fine. The chilling north wind roamed the more-slippery-than-a-divorce-lawyer narrow pathway and the downpour left you with no option of walking slow. Ioli and I walked arm in arm and wobbled along like an old couple in a rush to see the evening news.

'I hate mornings without a sun,' Ioli grunted.

I nodded in agreement while using all my strength to keep our umbrella from snapping or flying away over the rooftops a la Mary Poppins.

The church's white dome became visible through the falling drops. I remembered it being blue. One of the few memories my ten year old self managed to retain from the cruise around the Greek Islands with my then youthful parents. It is funny the things *we choose* to remember. So many things come and go, and unimportant things stay. A blue dome, falling off my bike outside Mr. Johnson's house, the day Peggy Anderson let one go in class, a scary clown from Twin Peaks. Random images, imprinted in our hard drive. I remembered the dome because right outside the church, amongst Japanese tourists living up to their photomania cliché, I asked my father why every island we visited had white painted houses and buildings. Sebastianos, stood up straight, uncrossed his arms and the lecture began. I never dared to interrupt him. He looked so proud spreading his knowledge and his love for his country with his ignorant more-American-than-Greek offspring.

'You feel all that sweat on your forehead and under your armpits? It's hot, Costa. Really hot. White reflects the harsh summer sun. It is heat resistant and that is why people across the Cyclades paint their homes bright white. And once a year, mainly before Easter, folks re-whitewash their houses and shops. Asbestos is cheap, too. White paint wasn't introduced until after World War One and it cost too much for the –then- fishermen and farmers.' He leaned closer to me and lowered his tour guide voice.

'Actually, Santorini never really followed tradition and used to have many colorful houses. Since the military Junta took over and orders were sent to maintain the Greek traditions and style, everyone painted white and added blue to show what great Greek patriots they were!' I had heard about the Junta before. It was the main topic in Astoria during the late sixties, right up until the mid-seventies, when a tank in Athens ran over some brave students and Turkey invaded Cyprus. That was the end of the dictatorship and the beginning of freedom in the land that gave birth to democracy.

'It's open,' Ioli shouted over. She pushed open the wooden door and entered the little church. Loud thunder shook the air as I entered, making me smile at the coincidence of timing. Cool air lingered inside. Modern houses had nothing on Greek buildings built during centuries long gone. Especially here in Santorini, where, to the Greek mixture of stone, wood, mud and hay, volcanic ash was added, working as cement.

The iconostasis stood small and humble. Still made of gold, but unpretentious compared to the grand scale ones, found in the newest built churches. The walls had recently been freshened up, with paintings of the evangelists and Bible scenes giving color to the dimly lit place. In front of the six rows of wooden stools, stood an elderly woman. She buzzed around the sand pit that served as a candle holder, emptying burnt out candles. The faithful visitors made a wish, said a prayer and lit a candle.

We walked over and stood behind her. She did not react.

'Excuse me?' Ioli raised her voice.

Startled, the woman dressed in a washed-out black skirt and a whiskey colored, high-neck blouse turned around.

'Oh my lord, you scared me. I left my hearing aid at home and did not hear you enter. Welcome to Agios Minas, blessed may be His name!'

'We are here to see the priest,' I said. More a question than a statement. We did not even bother to find out his name. Mother's call last night threw me off course. I skipped breakfast with Ioli -who never skipped any meal- and the lack of coffee had started taking its toll. I felt drained of energy. The alcohol swimming around my insides did me no favors either.

Ash grey eyes looked up into mine.

'He is on his way. Rain must be delaying him.' She paused. 'Who are you, sir?'

'I am Captain Costa Papacosta and this is...'

'Speak up boy.'

'AND THIS is Lieutenant Ioli Cara. We are with the Hellenic police.'

'Constantino!'

'Excuse me?'

'Your name is Constantino. Do not butcher it. It is offensive to Saint Constantino.'

I was ready to answer, but she had already shifted her round eyes over to Ioli.

'And Ioli! What kind of a name is that? You have no saint, thus no name day!'

'It is ancient Greek. The church itself declares and wishes for the continuation of Greek names. To maintain Greek tradition. Anyway, my mother always held me a name day celebration on the first Sunday after the Pentecost. The Holy All. Besides, if we stopped using certain names because there is no saint, how will those names end up with a saint? Someone has to be first, right? If Agios Mina's mother did not name him Mina because there wasn't a saint with that name, this church wouldn't be here.'

Never argue with an intelligent woman. Never.

The old lady was taken aback. Clearly not used to receiving a reply to her grunts. An answer began boiling inside her.

'Now listen here, young girl...'

'Why did they paint the dome white? I remember it blue. It was lovely,' I spoke simultaneously and drowned out her intro to a rant.

'Huh?'

'THE DOME. WHY DID THEY PAINT IT WHITE?'

'No need to shout. I'm not deaf, you know.'

'Could have fooled me,' Ioli whispered from behind closed teeth.

'Churches should be white.'

'It was better blue. The tourists loved it.'

'Well, we don't bend over to the tourists, Mister Constantino. It should be white.'

'I liked it blue, too.' A calm voice came from the door. 'Good morning, Helen.'

'Good morning, Father,' Helen replied, her face the color of new brick. 'Constantino and Ioli here are with the police,' she continued as she walked over to him. 'I'll be off now. Everything is clean. Keep it that way.'

'Yes, a good time to go. The rain has slowed down to a light drizzle,' he said with a warm smile. He watched her leave and locked the door behind her.

With the same warm smile still gracing his youthful-for-a-sixty-year-old face, he approached us. His smile was semi-hidden amongst his untrimmed, silver beard. The thick, wiry hairs formed a grey cone. His green eyes, full of life, gained your attention. You could feel them piercing through you, reading you, studying you.

'Sit, my children.' His hand inviting us to the wooden chairs. He took off his black kalimavxion, the chef type hat or chimney pot hat -if you prefer- that all Greek priests wear. He fixed his black robes; drops of rain soaking in. He finally sat down beside us. He extended his hand. Large cracked knuckles and gnarled fingers like the limbs of an ancient olive tree. Priests never extend their hand, in a handshake sort of way. It is more in a Victorian lady like way. I think it is their way of separating the crowd into believers and non-believers. The first kiss the hand, asking for their blessing, the latter turn it into an awkward handshake. Two such handshakes and name introductions later, I asked, 'Father Avgoustino, we are here to ask for your help. We have four dead people and we believe all attended church here. Can I show you some pictures and maybe you can tell us their story?'

'No need for gruesome pictures. Names will be fine. I know everyone who comes here. Besides, I watch the news and people in small societies talk too much. This is about Katerina, Mario and Stella. Who is the fourth, you refer to, I do not know.' His voice, calm, with a steady rhythm, relaxing. With a voice like that, you can say anything and make it sound sensible and logical. Unlike most Mediterranean men, his hands stayed still, one above the other on his lap. No arm waving to explain something. No body language, none at all. His body still, below his black clothes. I always wondered how they coped with the unbearable heat of the summer. Now, in the winter, it looked fine. In contrast to other Christian priests, Orthodox priests haven't changed their attire for the last thousand years or so. Many attribute this to tradition. Priests themselves say it is to mourn the Fall of the Great City, Constantinople. A fall that signalled the end of Byzantion, the Great Orthodox Empire. Historians declare that they were forced to wear black by the Ottomans who ruled Greece for four hundred years. Either way, slave clothes or not, mourning clothes or not, thousands of priests suffer every summer.

'John Mina,' Ioli filled in the seconds my mind took to ponder about his voice.

His eyes opened wide and his jaw dropped, taking his heavy beard with it.

'John's dead?' His voice trembled.

'Murdered yesterday at his workplace.'

'Yesterday? He was here yesterday morning...' the old man said and withdrew into his thoughts.

'Why was he here yesterday?' I asked.

'Confession.' He said no more. We knew he was not allowed to say any more. What was said stayed between them and God. Ioli spoke first.

'Father, we understand that you have confidentiality rules, but if he confessed to a crime and that crime got him killed, you have to help us. His killer is still out there.'

'Confess to a crime? What makes you say that?'

Ioli looked at me and I nodded. 'We believe he shot Kate Spanou.'

'No! John?'

'His rifle was the one used. What did he say, Father?'

'You love your job, don't you, young lady? There is a fire in your soul, and believe me, I understand you want to catch John's killer. I want you to catch him, too. However, there is no way I am uttering a single word from confession.'

'But he's dead.'

'His soul is still very much alive though. Besides, that is not the point. If people knew their dirty laundry might be revealed after death, how many do you think would be in here, opening up their hearts to me?'

Ioli sat back, defeated. The old guy had a good point.

'Well, Father, we know all four came here. I see you are a good priest that cares for his flock. How about we make a deal? I tell you a story and if I am right, you don't say a word.'

'He that has eyes to see and ears to hear may convince himself that no mortal can keep a secret. If his lips are silent, he chatters with his fingertips; betrayal oozes out of him at every pore.'

'Which Evangelist wrote this?'

He smiled. 'Freud.'

'You are quoting Freud to me?'

'My silence will be betraying. A false witness will not go unpunished, and he who breathes out lies will not escape.'

'Now, that I'm sure is from the Bible.'

'Proverbs, 19:5. You bring me to an awkward position, Captain. Tell me your story and I'll see what I can do. No word from confession will be part of my answer.'

'Kate found out that her husband, Mario, was cheating on her with Stella. She killed her husband; made it look like a heart attack. Somehow, Stella found out and this led to her death. Maybe, Stella paid John or used his gun to take the heat off her.'

'But she killed herself, no?'

I did not want to reveal that she was murdered.

'Guilt goes a long way.'

He closed his eyes. He remained still.

'I cannot help. I give you my blessings and may our Lord help you to shine light into your darkness. Have a nice day.' He got up quickly and walked away. We were left alone.

'Well, that was helpful,' Ioli remarked.

'He knows.'

'I bet he knows the whole story, but fuck if that helps us.' She turned towards Christ. 'Sorry.' She looked back at me. 'If mama knew I swore in church...' She ran her index finger across her throat.

Chapter Twenty-Six

Alexis Callis awoke later than usual. Much later than the dawn awakenings he had grown used to. He felt drawn to the sunrise. People were always amazed, and clapped at fireworks that lived only for a second in the night sky, but he had never seen anyone clap at a sunrise. So, he did. He woke up every morning and sat on his porch swing and clapped at the sunrise. Every day, the *painting* rose before his eyes. Every day with a different variety of colors.

A retired art teacher with a deceased wife and no kids to speak of (his dear Martha could not bear children and that was fine by him), he had nothing but time. Time to do what he loved. See the sunrise, garden, cook, watch awful TV shows, get drunk at all hours and...

...and make sweet, tender love to dead bodies.

Alexis always knew he was different. Always.

Many decades back, a wounded cat found refuge in his nursery's playground. It died during the cold, winter night. The next day, a group of preschoolers stumbled upon its body. All the kids screamed with horror and ran behind

Miss Kyriaki's flowery dress. She slowly walked around the thick oak tree, to witness a three year old Alexis holding the dead cat in his arms, cuddling it with tenderness shown to a newly-bought teddy bear.

During his teenage years, a time when all boys get their first boners, either by thinking of a specific girl or any pair of boobs, he got his first by thinking of the old lady next door. She had died and he had seen her lifeless body being carried away. The week after, he had his first wet dream. He awoke in frigid sweat and with a gooey substance on his lower belly. He cried from guilt. He had dreamt of sneaking in the morgue and raping a young girl's body. He was thrusting away; gazing in her hollow eyes.

Young Alexis never acted on his impulses.

His own thoughts sickened him to his core. He fought hard to be normal. At college, he asked Easy Voula out on a date. Voula was the sort of girl that declared girls should not put out until the fourth date, but always screwed on the first. A virgin Alexis sat nervously in his car as Voula waited for his move. He kissed and groped her. His penis paid no attention to his actions. It took Voula, who was always up for a challenge, ten minutes into an expert blow job to get him hard. She was well repaid for her efforts. Used to six minutes-then-explode twenty year olds, the half an hour Alexis spent inside her, pleasantly surprised her. In the end, Alexis could not take it anymore. He closed his eyes, thought of the dead girl from his dreams and came all over Voula's gravity defying boobs. That was his last piece of proof.

He was not normal.

After college, he married shy good little Christian girl Martha for *society's eyes*, for the sake of acceptance. It shut his mother up, well and proper. He slept with Martha twice a week and every Saturday with a corpse. He lied about a late night art lesson. He stole corpses from the village grave-yard and kept them in his shed, out in his grandfather's field. He kept them for a while, had his fun and returned them to their resting ground.

Today, he awoke late. He prepared his morning coffee, put on his dark green robe and stepped outside to inspect his garden. Yesterday's heavy rain worried him. His baby tomatoes were sensitive. He stood outside, glad of the now clear sky. The morning rain came and went. His shadow, a mere puddle around his feet. The midday sun floated in the canvas sky.

Yesterday, he killed for the first time.

It shocked him how easy it was to kill John. He watched the blood flow out of him. Ready and eager to leave, it came to him. A twisted epiphany. John was alive no more. He was a corpse, just like all the rest. He happily discovered a condom in his wallet and smiled at his luck. It was the warmest dead body he had ever been inside of. He came within minutes.

Just the thought of the previous day got him aroused. He soon realized little Alexis was peeking out from his robe, tall and proud. He ran inside, closing the door behind him. He dropped his robe to the tiled floor. He masturbated. Twice.

The rest of the day, what was left of it, passed by uneventfully. He cooked himself a terrific English breakfast. He had studied for a year in London and while he hated the British cuisine in general, he fell for the rich flavored break-fast. Since then, he indulged himself in milky black tea, juicy back bacon, fatty sausages, scrambled eggs and baked beans on toast. He then painted for a while, took a hot shower that left his skin rosy red and naked as he was, he fell on the sofa and turned on the TV. Five hours later and he decided on a jog, down at the beach. He dressed warm; you did not want a cold at his age. The bugs never leave you.

A black-sand beach, Monolithos beach, stretched for miles. In the summer, families roamed the area. Now, it lay deserted.

The sound of the waves echoed through the valley and hit against the tall rocks that ran along the beach. The weak sun reached its lowest point and the watermelon slice of a moon had already appeared in the sky.

Alexis gazed around him, taking in the colors and the serenity. He took in one deep breath for dramatic effect and began to jog. The wind, though calm, flew around icy. He tried to think where he had read that the cold was supposed to be good for you. It sure did not feel like that.

The orange color faded from the sky. The sun had half dipped into the Aegean Sea when he sensed that he was not alone. He stopped. He looked around. Apart from a few noisy seagulls and a couple of fishing boats on the horizon, he stood alone. He continued his run when he heard a twig snap.

'Hello?' He approached the bushy Acacia tree next to the rocks. The tree shook.

'Why are you following me? Come out! I must warn you that I used to box in college.' He tried to keep his voice from shaking.

'Really?' A deep voice came from right behind him. A rock hit him on the back of his head. He fell to the ground unconscious.

He woke up, five minutes later, a result of the icy water splashed on his face. Blindfolded and tied up, he lay on the ground.

'Let me go, please, why are you...'

'Shut the fuck up, you old pervert!' The same deep voice. It echoed as if they were in a small, closed space. Maybe one of the many little caves along the beach.

'Ready to pay for your sins?' a soft, whispery voice asked, from lips right next to his ear.

He fought to move, but he was tied down well. He felt two hands pull down his track suit bottoms.

'Ugh, the nasty fuck doesn't wear underwear,' the whispery voice said, getting louder.

For a moment, Alexis got excited at the idea of this being a sexual attack. He was always up for new things.

'Open your mouth,' ordered the soft voice. He did. But what he felt in his mouth was a hard piece of wood.

'That should keep him quiet,' the deep manly voice said, followed by sadistic laughter. 'Bring me the acid.'

'Say goodbye to your nasty necrophiliac cock!'

The sizzling sound of the acid gave his attackers shivers down their spines. They enjoyed watching him scream in silence. Alexis's eyes were at their largest and tears of pain formed a steady flowing river down his cheeks. The wood served its purpose well. They were alone on the beach, however they could not risk upsetting the quiescent bats.

'Let's put him out of his misery.'

That was the last thing Alexis ever heard. They both stabbed him with broken beer bottles left by teenagers and love-making couples in the cave. His throat was torn open and his chest disappeared under a pool of blood.

Chapter Twenty-Seven

I awoke drained. Even the gossamer hotel pillow could not prevent my neck from aching. We had spent the previous day processing the crime scene in the cave. Lights were set up, bats were forced to stay outside and we worked until the clock struck three in the morning. Ioli looked worse off than me. She always took pride in not being one of *those* women who act helpless during *those* days of the month. But now, every muscle in her body vibrated beneath her skin. Her period, once a steady flow for a couple of days, seemed to drag on and on. On top of all, her throat felt sore and her nose gave the first signs of a cold.

Today was not going to be any easier.

While we were in the cave, Constable Christina had visited the victim's house. Everything looked normal, as normal as an art teacher's house could be, but the stench from upstairs, smelled anything but normal. The whole house reeked of death. With her gun extended in front of her, Christina slowly walked up the stairs. She stood in shock, having pushed open the door of the master bedroom. Sitting up in bed, dressed in new clothes, lay a woman's corpse. A very old corpse. Blood had not flown through her for months; her dark purple skin had disintegrated to the bone. Eyes and hair were long gone and her remaining nails were ready to fall off.

A video recorder was set up, all alone on the bedside table. Calm as she could be in such a situation, Christina wore her gloves and picked up the device. Moments later, she had regretted pressing play. Alexis Callis had filmed all his sexual encounters with his dead companions. Christina's stomach could not handle anymore. She ran to the toilet and released her previous dinner, fish and mashed potatoes. The video kept on playing. An over excited Alexis Callis came all over the corpse's face, gave it a gentle kiss and carried the body away.

'You were good, baby! Another one for my yard collection!' he joyfully said.

Yes, today was not going to be any easier.

Today, we and the local police were going to dig up the old man's garden. Soon, we were going to be faced with all the bodies he did not return.

The uncomfortable silence was broken only by the sound of our shovels. No one spoke. Maybe, we were all too afraid of losing our breakfast in front of strangers.

Ioli dug away. She seemed the toughest, yet her insides screamed in disgust. It sickened her to the core that someone would steal a body from its resting ground and violate it in such a gruesome manner.

We pulled twelve bodies out of the soil, most tangled up amongst tomatoes and carrots. Eight women, three men and a teenager. The teenager was the last straw for Ioli. She cursed as she walked far away from the scene and headed down to the beach. She sat on a large rock and let the tears loose. She cried, ignoring the postcard sky opposite her. Her tears had dried by the time I sat beside her.

'There's too much evil in the world,' she said, her make-up smeared in the corners of her eyes.

'And it's our job to lessen it by catching the bad guys.'

'But it never stops. It's like Lernaia Hydra. You chop one head off and two grow in its place. We have been here for a few days and body after body after body...' She exhaled deeply. 'And my mind is driving me crazy. In Chania, family and friends kept my mind away from my job. I feel like we are living *death* twenty four seven.'

'We are all driven crazy by our thoughts. I know what you mean. When I was married, no matter what my eyes saw during the day, I could always count on unwinding at home with Tracy and Gaby. Now, the job is all I have. And the longer you live alone, the right side of your brain speaks louder and more often to you. Don't stay single too long, Cara. Find yourself someone to go home to.'

'Last thing on my mind at the moment...'

Witnessing death and chasing murderers can haunt you for life. But Ioli Cara was one tough cookie. She would one day learn to balance this life with a married life.

Chapter Twenty-Eight

DR. ARIADNE METAXA'S OFFICE

'You talk with great admiration whenever you speak about Ioli,' Ariadne pointed out, stroking her chin.

'One of the finest human beings I have ever met,' I smiled.

'She is not your daughter.' She uttered the words and watched them take effect.

'I don't need to fill in the gap. I would have been drawn to Ioli and be fond of her, even if Gaby were still alive.'

'What about the gap Tracy left?'

'Probably, for the best, to be honest. I was married for over twenty years. Marriage has its ups and downs, and now I enjoy being alone.'

'You got married once. The idea of growing old with someone is not appealing to you anymore?'

I looked away. After Gaby's death, I had lost the will to live. I decided to dedicate myself to work, to my dangerous job. Leave this world, having done some good. Ariadne leaned forward, waiting for an answer.

'I'll grow old with my job.'

'That sounds normal to you?'

'What is *normal*?'

'I must admit that the boundaries of normal are forever changing. However, working yourself to death is not the best of plans.'

'For the time being, it's my only plan.'

'It's up to you to make more.'

Awkward silence.

'Shall I get back to the story?'

'Oh, yes. You skipped a part, though. How did you discover the necrophiliac's body in that cave?'

'I was going to get there. A fisherman called it in. From his boat, he saw two men attack another and drag him into a cave. He had no phone or radio, so he called it in half an hour later.'

'Not very clever of him to be out at sea with no means of communication.'

I shrugged. 'We visited the fisherman after leaving the beach. After we both had scalding showers and wore lavender-smelling clothes, that is. Anything to get rid of the smell of death.'

'How is it to have death, right there, in front of you?'

'It gets to you eventually. You never get used to it. You just learn to cope with it better.'

Chapter Twenty-Nine

The majestic winter sky sailed above. A bright spot for sore eyes that witnessed too much death. A few puffy clouds shined orange as they swam across the clear sky. The fisherman lived alone in a little wooden hut built on his field of olive trees, meters from the sea and his life's companion, his fishing boat. The gates were open and we drove in. He expected us, after having called in the attack. He sat on a green wooden bench, underneath a large towering centenarian olive tree. A familiar figure sat beside him.

I parked the car and wondered where their cars were. The fisherman, a grey haired man in his early fifties, jumped up and opened two picnic chairs opposite the old, rustic bench.

'Father Avgoustino,' I said and nodded him hello to the familiar figure.

'Captain, Miss Ioli,' his serene voice left his lips. 'I should be on my way. Christo needed someone to talk to. He felt bad, having not reported the attack earlier.'

'Maybe the good old teacher would still be alive,' Christo said.

'The good old teacher was a necrophiliac and had stolen bodies buried in his yard,' Ioli cut to the chase. Christo's huge turquoise eyes opened wide and his jaw fell to the ground. Disgust and disbelief painted Father Avgoustino's face. Both looked as if they had something to say, but had difficulty finding the right words. It's not every day that you learn about your neighbor's secret life.

'Can I offer you something to drink?' the fisherman kindly asked. Ioli and I both refused with a shake of the hand and a faint smile.

'Father?'

'I must be going, my child. The hour is late and I have to be at the homeless shelter for dinner time.'

'Are there many homeless?' Ioli asked.

An island of 17000 with a homeless shelter?

He smiled and looked up to meet the tall girl's brown eyes. 'No, thank God. We just call it that. Only a couple of people staying there, but we run it for all. We feed many families in need. Now, with the crisis, things are tight for everyone. I make sure they know Jesus is there for them.'

She nodded with apathy and turned to sit down.

'Maybe you would like to come, my child?' he continued.

'Who? Me?' Ioli asked, slightly confused.

'Yes. You have a storm going on in your soul. Many things tormenting you. Helping others is the best therapy.'

'Thanks for the offer, but I have work. I help others by catching the real evil ones out there.'

'Too much death, too much evil for such young eyes. Don't let Satan get the best of you. Have a good evening,' he said, bowed his head and turned. Ioli watched in silence as the old man walked up to the main road.

'Is he walking back to town?' I asked the fisherman.

'Oh, yes. Father Avgoustino always walks. Keeps him healthy. He says our body was given to us by God and we must respect it. It is our temple in which He resides.' He looked up and made sure Father Avgoustino was out of sight. 'And now he is gone, I can fill up my temple with some Assos smoke.' He placed the cigarette between his lips. He spoke as he lit the little delicious cancer stick. 'My grandfather used to work for Papastratos Tobacco back in the late forties. Finest Greek cigarettes, he used to say. Please, sit.'

'Christo, you called the police station around nine o'clock last night. But you said that you had been out at sea. What time did the incident take place? What exactly did you see?'

He took in more Assos smoke. His cigarette came alive at its end, glowing red. He exhaled a dark cloud of smoke that scattered in the light breeze and headed to sea.

'It must have been near eight. I am not sure how far out I was, but I have good eyes, I can assure you. I was daydreaming, watching the shore getting further and further away. I saw a man jogging along the beach. I was ready to turn and captain my boat to deeper waters, when I saw two men jump him and hit him over the head. The man fell to the ground and they picked him up and took him into one of those little caves behind the beach. I cursed when I realized that I had left my cell phone at home...' He bowed, ashamed to look us in the eye. 'I... I thought of the price of gas and I did not want any trouble, so at first I headed out to sea, but I couldn't fish. My mind was on the attack. I felt bad as a human, you know? So, I returned to shore, drove home and called the police.' He lifted his shaking right hand and saw that his cigarette was just a line of ash. He threw it aside and lit another.

'Don't beat yourself...' I started to say, but Ioli had no time for a comfort talk.

'Can you describe the two men, Mr. Christo?' she asked.

'Well... Not really. I was quite far out. Two shadowy figures attacking another. All I can say is that one was much larger than the other. Both in height and in weight.'

'Color of clothes? Type of clothes?'

'All looked dark as the sun dipped in the ocean. Probably wearing jeans or trousers.' His smoke came my way. I was getting annoyed with my smoking addiction for teasing me. I thought I had beaten it. Now, I was craving a cigarette so badly. I felt like a chocoholic tied to a chair watching as everyone walked past him, Nutella jar in hand. I tilted my chair backwards and took a deep breath of clean air. The fresh air from the lemon trees around us gave me a sense of healthy living and kicked my craving to the curb. Now, if only it would stay there.

'If you remember anything, call me at once,' Ioli said politely, passed him her card and got up. By the time I had shaken his hand, she was already behind the steering wheel, eager to get back to the scene. She had *the itch*. All investigators get it. You get too close to your case and you cannot relax until your case is closed. Even then it is hard letting go.

Chapter Thirty

A good detective is nothing without a good lab team; truth must be said. Before the advance of technology, many cases were left unsolved or worse, the wrong person took the heat. Great investigators lived back then, but sometimes, brains weren't enough.

The next day, Ioli and I stood above a table of evidence and a bunch of new results from Athens' lab. We pretty much knew the story. Now we had the backing of DNA and fingerprints. A wife drugged her cheating husband, a carpenter shot her and hung the mistress, a necrophiliac murdered the carpenter and two attackers brutally killed the necrophiliac.

'Someone is orchestrating this...' I whispered, leaning over the gruesome pictures. Each murderer getting murdered by the next.

'An evil mastermind? How...' Ioli started to ask before shouting out 'Bingo!'

'What?'

'Well, why didn't I open you first?' she asked, holding a

brown envelope sent from our labs. 'The hairs collected from the necrophiliac were identified. He's in the system. Andrew Kontos. Age 17. He got into a serious bar fight last year and was arrested.'

'Let's go pay Andrew a visit, then.'

'You don't sound pleased.'

'Well, it's not evidence that will hold up in court. He could say, he was in the cave with a girl or with mates the previous day. We need to get hard evidence...'

'Or a confession! Come on, let's go and get this kid's story.'

The weather continued behaving like my ex during her pregnancy. One day all bright, the next dark and gloomy. The sun had taken the day off. The sky was painted charcoal black all over. The clouds had united into one big menacing carpet and began pouring it down.

The Kontou house rose in front of us, at the end of a z-shaped country road, just on the outskirts of the capital. Farms of decades past, gave way to two-storey homes built by developers to house the younger generation of home buyers. Couples looking for a nest for their love to bloom and to bring offspring into the world. Couples like Maria and George Kontou. Now, in their early forties and parents of two boys and two girls. The oldest being Andrew, our newly found suspect.

I parked outside the Kontou family home and dreaded the long run up to the door.

'Want the blue or the black umbrella?' Ioli asked, leaning to the back seats where she had placed the borrowed items from the police station.

'You are a star,' I said, using my grandma's line. Ioli gently punched me on my shoulder.

'And don't you ever forget it. I'll take the blue one. Meet

you at the door.' She leaped out the car, slamming the door behind her. The howling wind pulled her a few steps forward as she opened her umbrella. She cursed the rain and then after stepping into a muddy puddle, she cursed again. I had more success, my weight able to defy Borea's gusty, blustery attacks.

We stood under the protection provided by the front porch pergola. The loud television and childrens' laughter filled the house. After catching her breath, Ioli rang the doorbell.

'Turn that TV down you two,' a woman's voice commanded. Her voice brought on no change to the ongoing noise pollution. *Barbie in Fairytopia* kept on booming. The brown wooden door opened to reveal a forty-year-old housewife. She looked like she had been yanked out of a fifties washing powder commercial; with her curly hair tied up with an orange bandana, her nails painted red, her white apron tied around her waist and flat shoes covering her feet. She held a duster and wore a wide, bright smile. Until she saw us. Taken aback, her smile faded and her lips fell flat. Saturday morning as it was, she expected it to be a neighbor, ready for a hot Greek coffee and even hotter and steamier gossip.

'What is it with Jehovah Witnesses and Saturday mornings? Can't you see the sticker?'

The oval sticker on her door warned: ORTHODOX CHRISTIANS LIVE HERE. NO VISITS BY JEHOVAH WITNESSERS OR MEMBERS OF OTHER HERESIES. More instructions followed on the next sticker. NO DOOR TO DOOR SALES.

'Not here to preach or sell,' Ioli replied dryly.

'Hellenic Police, ma'am. I am Captain Costa Papacosta and this is Lieutenant Ioli Cara. Is your son Andrew home?'

Her eyes widened and flashed in the same way a lioness' would if you went near her cubs. 'What do you want with my boy?'

'We are here to question him about his whereabouts yesterday. Is he home? Can we come in and talk?' I asked.

'Come in,' she said reluctantly after a second or two. We followed her into the living room, where two girls were dancing away. They both froze at the sight of strangers. Maria Kontou switched the TV off and ordered them to their room.

'And tell Andrew to get his ass down here! Now!' Normally the girls would have giggled at the sound of the word ass, but something in their mother's tone warned them that this was not a laughing matter. Maria opened a large side window overlooking the back yard and called out to her husband to bring the same body part as her son's into the house too. George Kontou spent his morning in the shed, tidying up his tools at his wife's command. Maria's strong voice had no trouble traveling through the rain, defying the downpour and the thunder, and reaching her husband's ears. In a matter of minutes, introductions were made, lemonade and coffee were offered and a guilty-looking teen sat between his parents on the well-worn family sofa. We sat on two high back armchairs opposite them.

Andrew was a very tall, thin, light brown haired kid. He stood out between his much shorter parents. His two large turquoise eyes shined like gemstones amongst his acne-ridden face. He placed his hands on his lap and could not stop scratching his knuckles. He took one look at us and for the rest of the time, kept his eyes focused on the floor. If guilty needed a picture for the dictionary, Andrew would be it.

'Andrew, you have nothing to fear,' Ioli tried to calm the

youth down with a friendly smile. 'We only want to know your whereabouts yesterday late evening.'

'What do you think he has done?' his father asked, but Ioli paid no attention to him. She tilted her head and tried to make eye contact with the boy.

'Hanging around with friends.' His voice fought to come out and we strained our ears to hear him better.

'Where?' I asked, while his father angrily told him to speak up.

'At the park. The one behind the old supermarket...'

'And where else?'

'Nowhere really, miss. Stayed there for hours, we did. Then drove around town. I was home by eleven. My mama saw me come in...' Maria nodded in agreement and stroked her boy's back.

'Why are you so anxious, Andrew?' I asked.

'I don't know what you want.'

'What do you think this is about?'

He looked at his father and bowed his head, even lower.

'Weed.'

'What?' his mother cried out.

'Had some fun at the park, did you, Andrew?'

'I... I only smoked a bit. I don't know who brought it. It was just passed around for fun. We are not dealers or anything.'

His father looked confused.

'You came to our house about a teenager having a smoke? You aren't local police. Why are you here? We have rights, you know.'

'I know, sir. I just wanted to give your son a chance to declare his whereabouts. We are investigating a murder case...'

'A murder case!' Maria Kontou looked stressed out and

ready to faint. Her face turned pale white, drained of all color, and her head shook from side to side in denial. 'No, no. My boy has nothing to do with any murder. He was at the park...' she mumbled away, not sure how to continue her sentence.

'What murder case?' his father wanted to know.

'Alexis Callis'.

'The retired art teacher?' Maria asked.

'That's the one. He was murdered down by Monolithos beach, in one of the little caves along the beach,' I said.

'And why do you think my son has anything to do with this?'

'Mr. Kontou, your son's hair were found on the body,' Ioli stated. Maria could not hold back her tears. George stared at his son in disbelief. The youth stood up and raised his voice.

'Now you listen here. I was at the park with my friends. I have nothing to do with this. I did not even know the guy. This is crazy.'

'Sit down, please,' Ioli said and his parents gently pulled him back to the sofa. 'No one is making any accusations here. We are investigating evidence. How did your hair end up on the body of Alexis Callis?'

'I don't know. We hang about in those caves often. Always have. All teenagers go down there, to drink, smoke... be with a girl, you know?'

As I predicted. The answer we did not want to hear. The evidence was circumstantial at best.

'You can't blame my boy for this shit, pardon my language. The guy was murdered in a cave where Andrew had sat with his friends. It's the same as finding a dead guy at my work. I'm sure many of my hairs are on the bank's floor.'

'As I said, we are only following leads. Thank you for your time,' I said and got up. Ioli stared at me for a good minute. She stood up beside me and whispered in my ear. 'That's it? We are not pushing it more?'

'Let's talk in the car.' I turned towards Andrew. 'Names of friends who can verify you were at the park last night.'

'Erm, who was there? Christo, Annita, Alina, Costa... I think Emily was there for a while, Antony came later and stayed till late... There was a bunch of others too, but these are the ones I was with.'

'Your story better check out or we will be back. Have a nice day.'

We left behind a distressed family and a grounded-for-a-month Andrew.

'Weed? You stupid boy.' His mother slapped him across his face. Never mess with an angry Greek mother. Never. Andrew took the walk of shame up to his room. Sexting with Alina would relax his mind. In the meanwhile, Ioli's mind could not relax.

We drove off in silence. Minutes later, I turned to Ioli, lost in her thoughts. 'The evidence isn't...'

'Enough to stand up in court. I know. That is why I knew we needed a confession. Just disappointed, that's all. Pay no attention to me, my body and my mind have ganged up against me lately. I'll be fine.'

And when Ioli stressed that she will be fine, that signaled the end of the conversation. She hated being asked if she was okay. She once told me 'and what is *okay* anyway? This is a crazy world we live in. I don't think we are ever okay. By what criteria are we okay? And what an annoying word! *OK*... So simple, so shallow...'

The weather for once decided on being our ally. The downpour, had turned into a mizzle and, by evening, the clouds had vanished from the sky. The winter sun was off early to bed and all the Thira teens came out to play. The park filled up with bike-riding teens, young boys on roller skates trying hard to impress the girls with their moves and groups of five or six gathered around benches, smoking, drinking and laughing.

It did not take long to find Andrew's gang. Everyone knows everyone in small towns. First kid we asked, pointed towards where the ones we were looking for were sitting. As we approached the group, their vibrant talking diminished into silence. They all turned, curiosity mixed with uncertainty written in their eyes. They did not get to see many strangers during the winter.

'Hey,' Ioli approached, smiling. 'Nice wheels.'

'Thanks,' Antony answered, sitting up straight on his black BMX.

'We were wondering if you could help your friend Andrew out. We are with the police and...'

With the sound of the word police, they all straightened up and exchange worried looks.

'... we need to note down Andrew's whereabouts so he isn't blamed for something he did not do. He was here with you last night, right?'

Annita spoke first. She spat out her chewing gum and said that Andrew was at the park last night.

'What time did he get here?' I asked.

'Around six. There was still light,' Christo said. 'It was just the three of us in the beginning, but soon we were all here. Is Andrew in trouble, sir?'

'Not if you can verify that he was here with you. And you sat here all night?'

'Well, mostly, yeah.'

'We went to the kiosk at one point.'

'I left early...'

'I left and came back around ten...'

'Did Andrew leave at any point?' Ioli asked, interrupting the simultaneous answers.

'Erm, I don't think so,' an unsure Emily said.

'He was here, when I got back at eleven,' Costa said.

His breath smelled of marijuana. A plastic bag with a couple of bottles of alcohol lay by the side of the bench. These teens came here for what they perceived to be a good time and got wasted. Desultory teenagers came and went. Andrew could have left, returned later, and still have witnesses verifying he had been there the whole time.

'We have two options,' Ioli said as we walked back to the car. 'We either accept that Andrew had nothing to do with the murder and his hairs were already in the cave or we accept that this park is the best alibi ever. Dozens of kids coming and going at all hours, not looking at the clock. He could have left at seven and come back at half past eight and still have witnesses.'

My thoughts exactly.

I tried hard to keep my thoughts on the case. It was hard not to think of my father being hit by a car and lying in a hospital bed. I texted relatives as often as I could. To get updates on his condition, but mostly to see how my mother was coping. I could not find the courage to talk to her. I know my decision outraged her. I hoped that one day she would understand.

A dark night surrounded us. No visible moon and the majority of stars had yet to come out to play. We drove down dark streets where the cold wind blew. Everyone, besides the crazy youngsters in the park, locked up warm in their homes.

'Watch out,' Ioli screamed and I slammed down on the

brakes. A black figure ran out into the street. The tires screeched, leaving behind black snake-like lines on the road. We came to a halt; the car's lights revealing Father Avgoustino as he froze like a cat in the middle of the street. His eyes were wide open, in obvious shock. His black clothes were soaked in blood and drops fell from open wounds on his head. He breathed frantically.

'Help me... Help me,' he kept repeating, each time the words coming out louder and louder. He gathered his courage as he realized who we were. We stepped out of the car and approached him. He fell to his knees.

'Thank God, it's you. He is in the church. He tried to kill me.' He lifted his finger and pointed towards the alleyway that led to the church. 'Get him,' he said and collapsed.

Chapter Thirty-One

DR. ARIADNE METAXA'S OFFICE

'Were you close? Your father and you?' Ariadne Metaxa asked. She had just placed my herbal tea next to me on a wooden hand-carved side table.

I sunk back into the soft armchair. I forced a smile. 'Just because I did not drop everything and rush off to New York, doesn't mean we weren't close or I didn't care.'

She did not reply until she had poured her share of the pungent tea and sat down slowly in the armchair opposite me. 'Did I imply such a thing? Have I ever judged you, Costa?' She brought the steamy, porcelain teacup to her full lips. The moment she took her first sip, was probably one of the few moments her eyes were not focused on me.

'Mmm... I love a warm cup during these cold evenings...' Another passionate sip. 'Maybe a story, to complete the setting. I am sure, you have a good father and son tale to share.'

'We were as close as men were back then. He did not say I love you and we rarely hugged, but the love was there. I was his only son. You know, Greek parents back then had a saying. I have one child and two daughters.' She gave off her characteristic giggle.

'People with *just* daughters had no children then.'

'Something like that. He worked his ass off for his family. Mama too. Immigrants in a foreign land with a heavy accent and little knowledge of the language. He came back from the factory broken and went back every morning with a smile. We never felt poor. We never felt children of a lesser God. Father always provided. I am so proud of him. Always have been. He wasn't always there for me, but when I really needed him, I knew I could count on him. He taught me to ride a bike, to shave, to drive...'

A tear fought to form in the corner of my eye. Call me old fashioned, but men of my time, do not cry in front of pretty ladies. During Ariadne's next sip, the tears were quickly wiped away.

'As for your story... I must have been sixteen at the time, approaching seventeen. I started dating this Mexican girl from my biology class. She was drop dead gorgeous, smart, funny, but my mother would not approve. All us Greek kids had to find a *decent* Greek girl to date.' I rolled my eyes. 'Anyway, I did not say a word about Lucia at home. One Saturday evening, I found on my bed a ten dollar note and a piece of paper that said *take that girl somewhere nice.* The following week, more money and another note *buy her some-thing romantic like flowers or chocolates,* this time. Cliche, I know. This went on for like a month or so. I believed mama thought I was dating a Greek girl or that she was cooler than I had her out to be. So, one day, I came out the shower and on my bed was a box of condoms. The note read: *Costumes for your gentleman. Be respectful to the girl and don't worry too much. Big size dicks run in the family. She will be pleased!*'

Ariadne could not control her laughter. Her usual

ephemeral giggle, now a roaring laughter. 'You can't be serious?'

'Oh, I am. It was my dad all along. What made it even more embarrassing, was the next day when we were alone, he asked me how it went and started giving me tips how to change positions often and let the girl take control when she's on top and... it makes me wonder how it took me so long to end up in therapy!'

'He sounds like one hell of a guy.'

'Yeah, he truly was.'

Chapter Thirty-Two

Ioli pushed open the heavy wooden church door and leaped into the room with her gun stretched out, searching around. I ran around the church; it was deserted. Just us and the chilling breeze. Inside, Christ's large icon had been painted with Father Avgoustino's blood as the attacker had bashed his head against the icon multiple times. The elderly man crawled into the church on all fours, shaking all over, asking the Lord for His protection. Ioli sat down beside him. She calmed him and took a look at his deep scars. Paramedics were shortly by their side. Constable Christina appeared with them, forensic kit in her right hand.

'Just as you asked, Captain.' I had returned to the church after a run through the neighborhood. Not a single soul in the streets. The assailant had gotten away.

I took samples of the blood, though I knew it was unlikely that the fragile old priest had managed to fight back. I picked and bagged a few hairs too. The church was a public place and no help would be provided from analyzing them, but I had to be thorough.

'I'm going with the priest,' Ioli said. 'I'll try to get a statement as soon as he is ready.'

'Want me to go?'

'No, it's fine. I'm feeling better today and I need to prove to myself that I am back to being me! Anyway, old guys need their rest. Don't stay up too late.' She gave me a nudge on my shoulder and with her Julia Robert's smile upon her face, she was off.

I handed Christina the evidence and instructed her to send it immediately to the labs. Knees and back aching, I walked towards my car. A beer and a hot shower later, I was lying naked between the hotel's warm sheets. The TV was playing the usual crap, with re-runs of Turkish and Mexican soap operas dominating the late night scene. I left the less annoying one on.

'Oh, his eyes. His gorgeous blue eyes,' poor Juanita daydreamed over Prince Juan. As if the King and Queen would let their son marry a farmer's daughter.

Stupid show. As if the two brown-eyed royals could be the parents of the blue-eyed prince. It's more than rare that both carry the recessive gene of...'

I sat up. My heart skipped a beat and then began to race.

'Brown is a dominant color! Recessive blue, here in the Cyclades? Well, I'll be damned!'

I picked up my phone. I called -and woke up- the chief. I needed a warrant and I needed it fast.

'You have some balls, Costa, but if you think I am waking up a judge at one in the morning, you have another thing coming! There is no fleeing risk. Zero. Nada. Nyet. Go to sleep and by the time you wake, your warrant will be faxed to you.' That was the chief's way of letting me know, that a judge would be notified first thing in the morning and soon, our suspect would be in jail.

Chapter Thirty-Three

I had managed to log in a couple of hours of restless sleep. My mind, focused on the *game*, would not let my body relax. When I finally closed my eyes, my daughter came to my dreamland.

'Come on daddy, die already and come play with me,' she would giggle while murderers of cases past appeared around me, each killing me in their own gruesome way.

Ariadne is going to love this dream.

I woke up, covered in a cold sweat. I showered slowly, killing time until the Mediterranean sun came out of the ocean and sent its first rays through my open window. I dressed and sped next door to wake up Ioli. She had stayed up late too, working on Father Avgoustino's testimony. The priest did not get a chance to see his attacker. He recalled being ambushed and grabbed from behind. The attacker hit his head violently on the solid wood icon, blurring his vision and weakening his senses. The old man managed to kick the perpetrator in his privates and fled.

'Ioli? Get up, now. Quick!'

'What the... Costa, is that you? What are you, a fucking rooster or what? Jesus...' she kept on moaning and cursing, but I knew the act. I could hear her moving around, getting dressed.

'What?' she finally opened the freshly-painted maroon door.

'The kid's eyes are turquoise. Both parents have brown eyes.' I loved that I never had to say more with Ioli. Smartest partner I have ever had.

She took a second and said 'Brown is a dominating color. If one had brown and the other blue, it would be possible, yet rare. But two brown eyed parents with a blue eyed kid? That's one in a million. You think he is adopted? How does that connect to the case?'

'No, he's not adopted. I woke Christina last night and had her check hospital records. She cursed less than you, by the way. He is his mother's son alright. But that those blue eyes, the strong jaw, that nose, the height, the way his ears point out...'

'Oh my... The fisherman!'

'That's what has been on my mind! Spitting image aren't they? Got a warrant for the kid. We are bringing him in for questioning.'

'An unfaithful mother is not a crime.'

'Something's fishy about the fisherman. Pitiful excuses were all he had. If he was out to sea, how did he see the attack? And if he was close to shore, why didn't he come to land at once and report it? Or, at least, shout out to the attackers. He was safe on his boat. He took his time. My money is on him identifying his son and that's why he took his time. To give the boy time or maybe even warn him to plan an alibi.'

She smiled. A mysterious look graced her face.

'What?'

'Nothing. Just proud of you. I'm glad that you're my partner.'

Her words came unexpected and touching. I did not want to get emotional, so as always, I resulted to humor. 'Aw, I knew you were capable of being nice. Come here, give us a hug.'

'And the moment is gone. Fuck off. It's too early for hugs. Let's go get that kid.'

Outside the Kontou home, the whole family rushed around on their way out. The kids packed and ready for school, mother ready to drop them off, father ready for another 9 to 5 day. Smiles all around. Until they saw us, that is.

The father approached us, anger flashing in his eyes.

'Now, look here. Andrew is on his way to school. You have upset him enough with your accusations...'

'Step aside, sir,' Ioli said firmly and walked towards the tall, young man who look ridiculous hiding behind his petite mother.

'We have a warrant for your son's arrest,' I shocked the father.

'Andrew Kontou, you are requested to follow us to the station with a guardian, for further questioning. Refusal will lead to you being handcuffed. Please, follow me to the patrol car.'

His mother started crying, shaking her head from side to side. 'Stop them,' she cried out to her husband.

'Call your mother, to come get the kids, now! We are following them to the station. Control yourself for the kids' sake.'

Ioli opened the back door and helped Andrew in. The boy was shaking all over. Sweat formed all over his forehead. By the time, we reached the station, his blue T-shirt had stuck to his back and two pools of bodily fluids had taken shape under his armpits.

We escorted him to questioning room A. Weird name for a questioning room as the building had no other questioning rooms. I brought in more chairs in anticipation of his parents.

'Do you want anything to drink, Andrew?' Ioli asked. He shook his head, keeping his eyes glued to the white tile floor. 'Try to relax,' she advised the youth.

Constable Christina opened the door and in flew his mother, ready for her fifties-style, Greek movie scene.

'My boy, my sweet boy, you okay?' She hugged and kissed him on both cheeks.

'Mum, cut it out.' He turned a light shade of red. His father touched his son gently on the shoulder and sat down beside him. His mother took a second to stare around the room, before sitting down.

'Andrew, we checked out your alibi...' I began to say.

'I was at the park! Didn't my friends tell you that?'

'Boy, let the man speak,' his father ordered him, anxious to hear what I was going to say.

'Yes, you were at the park. But witnesses have all of your gang leaving at various times and no one could confirm that you were there from beginning to end.' His fingers came together and turned into fists. His breathing got louder.

'I was there.' He emphasized every word of his short statement.

'Were you married when Andrew was born?' Ioli asked, catching his parents off guard.

'Excuse me?' George Kontou asked.

'What kind of question is that?' Maria Kontou managed to ask. She was as pale as the white walls.

'The kind of question that requires an answer.'

'Yes, we were.'

'In what year of your marriage was Andrew born?' Ioli continued.

'Erm... What has any of this...'

'Can you answer the question, sir?'

'Six months after our wedding. Maria was three months pregnant on our wedding day.'

'Do any of you, know Christo Riga?'

Andrew's breathing got louder, his face acquired the coloring of a juicy, freshly cut tomato and his mother looked ready to pass out. Her eyes opened wide and her stare went from us to her husband like she was watching a ping-pong match.

'Who? The loner fisherman? I see him a couple of times at the coffee shop. What has he got to do with any of this?' the clueless man answered.

'Do you know him, Mrs. Kontou?' Ioli threw the question at the distraught woman.

Maria Kontou sat there, staring right at Ioli, lost for words.

'Mrs. Kontou?'

'I... I know him by name. We are a small island. Not like Athens here. We know each other...' she started mumbling away.

'So you have never met before?'

'No.'

'Mrs. Kontou. Christo Riga is an eye witness in a murder case. If we have reason to believe he gave false testimony, then we are obliged to check out the reasons why. We could even order a DNA test, if we have too,' Ioli said, lying through her teeth. Such a thing would be extremely difficult, but Ioli knew this was how we would get results.

'A DNA test?' George asked.

'This is outrageous! You cannot do such a thing, you have no right, I will never allow it!' Maria shouted, standing up. Ioli sat back in her chair. She had accomplished her mission.

George stared at his wife. 'Maria?' His voice was shaking. Andrew started to cry.

'Maria? What are you hiding?' He stood up and faced his wife. 'Speak to me!'

She had frozen. She could not utter a single word.

'Dad, please...'

'Don't you please me, boy. Maria, you better start talking or I swear to God, I will strangle you right here, in the police station.'

'Mama, don't...'

'George, I love you, You are my all. I can't stand this dirty secret any longer. Our fathers arranged our marriage. Christo was my lover at the time. When I found out that I was pregnant, I swear I believed the baby was yours. But, look at him...' She did not manage to say anything else. She watched as all the accumulative love vanished from her husband's eyes. A cold distant look painted his face.

'You disgust me. Are any of the children mine?'

'George! I have never been unfaithful to you! I conceived Andrew before our wedding. You think it was easy for me to forget, from one day to the next, my boyfriend at the time and start dating a new man, picked by my father?'

'Oh, fuck off. You're the victim now? You let me raise him as my own...'

'He is yours! You have always been his father, you...'

'He is no blood of mine. And you are not the woman I thought I had married,' he said and stormed out the room.

Maria ran after him. Their fighting continued all down the hall and out of the building.

'I love you,' Maria screamed, pulling her husband's T-shirt as he walked off. He turned and slapped her hard across the face, throwing her to the hard ground. Police officers rushed to hold him back and dragged him into a holding room to cool off. Christina helped Maria up and took her inside for a hot cup of tea and to offer a shoulder to cry on.

Meanwhile, inside, Andrew looked at us with blind fury in his eyes.

'Now, look what you have done! You have ruined my family. You have no shame...'

'How long have you known?' I asked.

'Since I was twelve. Christo approached me one day. Said he wanted to get to know me. I thought he was a pervert and threatened to call the cops. He said he was my biological father.' He laughed. 'I ran home crying. Mum was furious with him. She told me not to breathe a word to my father, as he had a weak heart and this would kill him. Stupid bitch. Who says that to a kid? Couldn't she have lied to me? Anyway, next time he approached me, I wanted to get to know him, you know? He was my father, after all. We would meet whenever we could. He is a great man. Better man than George could ever be. He taught me so much.'

'Taught you to kill?' Ioli asked.

'No, he...' He paused.

'You know that we are going to arrest him for giving a false testimony?'

'You can't do that...'

'And charge you with murder. Your alibi is weak and we have your DNA on the body...'

'You can't do this. My father is a good man. That priest

is to blame. What do you people call it? He was the abettor. He told my dad about that sick fucker. Sex with dead bodies. A Satanist that's what he was. God strikes down sinners and sometimes He needs a little help with His plans.'

'Your father told you that?'

'No. Father Avgoustino did. He told me that I was a bastard and God had no place in Heaven for bastards or sinners like my mother and biological father. He said, my father was brave and was going to do God's work by killing the necrophiliac. And that I should help him. Only then, would my mother and I be able to walk through heaven's gates.'

And just like that, Andrew's words worked like glue. All the pieces fell together and formed a clear picture. The mastermind behind all: Father Avgoustino. He listened to everyone's confessions and found out who the sinners were. Then, he manipulated them, to kill each other by promising them forgiveness and entry to heaven. He advised Kate to kill her husband and he persuaded the carpenter to kill both Kate and Stella. And after each kill, he had the next killer ready to take out the previous one. Alexis was sent to kill the carpenter, while the fisherman and his son would then kill Alexis.

Andrew's confession probably saved his life. The priest would have had someone lined up to continue his evil plan to eradicate all sinners.

The rain came and went in a matter of minutes. Light grey clouds wandered over the blue sky and the mild breeze brought a sense of freshness to the air. Ignoring the low temperatures we drove with the windows down. Nothing like a whiff of the Aegean Sea to make you feel alive. Nature gave birth to a rainbow ahead. Its blend of colors travelled from the horizon, up into the sky and vanished behind a group of clouds. Clouds conspiring to start raining again.

'Beautiful, isn't it?'

Ioli had relaxed. A closed case had that effect. I, on the other hand, felt my heart race. I always needed to make the arrest for closure to take place. Ioli needed sense. She needed to know, to solve. Then, she relaxed.

'It sure is,' I answered.

'This is the sign of the covenant that I make between me and you and every living creature that is with you, for all future generations. I have set my bow in the clouds; a sign of the covenant between me and the earth.'

'Excuse me?'

She laughed out loud, amused by my puzzled face. It felt good to hear her genuine laughter, once again.

'It's from the Bible. Genesis, I think.'

'And since when have you quoted the good book?'

'My grandma use to say it at the sight of every rainbow. I learnt it as a poem, never really understanding its meaning. At least, as a kid.'

'You think the earth and God are connected?'

'I think we are all connected. In one weird, messed-up way. I truly want to believe as I believed when I was a kid, but logic always ends up getting in the way.'

'Connected, huh?'

'Some people more than others. Take Father Avgoustino. A seemingly kind, old man, loved by his community, into charity and all, and he felt the need to kill. Or have people kill for him. Was he connected to God? No. But he surely felt he was.'

'I'm not sure I'm getting your point.'

'God or no God, it does not matter to me. It is all about

how you understand your place in the world, how connected you are. Connected enough to do what's right. Some people become so disconnected, they become dangerous to the rest.'

'And it's our job to stop them.'

'Yeah, two freaking guardian angels, aren't we?' she said with laughter.

The newly-built blue-painted hospital stood out amongst its surrounding two floor buildings. The glass doors came alive as we approached them. We took the elevator up to the fifth floor. The head nurse led us to his room.

'How is he?' I asked.

'His injuries are healing well. None were serious. It is the cancer that is keeping him weak.'

'Cancer?'

'Yes, ma'am. Stage three. At his age, it is a miracle he can still get around. It is a terrible burden to his old heart.'

We found him, frail in his hospital bed. Tubes came and went, and his heart monitor beeped through the silence. He managed to open his eyes.

'Well, hello there. How is the investigation coming along?'

'Great, we found out who your attacker was,' Ioli said. His eyes widened.

'Really?'

'Yes, you. You banged your head on that icon. A moment of frustration or an evil plan to throw us off track, I don't know. But, I do know, you were alone when you gained your injuries.'

He struggled to sit up. He exhaled deeply.

'Not evil, just an old fool's plan.'

'So, you're not denying it, then?' I asked.

'No reason in lying, now at the end of it all. How did you find out?'

'Andrew spoke. We have him down at the police station. Local police are arresting his father -his real father- as we speak.'

'Justice for all...' he said, coughing hard. His whole chest rocked back and forth.

'You believe you served justice?'

'God's justice.'

'Answer me this, Father,' I said. 'We have all the evidence. Just one clue missing. What was the carpenter's sin?

'Rape. During his time in the army, he raped a girl in a night club. Ever since, he has tried to receive God's forgiveness. I helped him get it.'

'You are responsible for all those deaths!' Ioli could not believe her ears.

'Deaths of sinners. God has punished sinners since the beginning of time, my child. Sodom and Gomorrah, ancient Egypt...'

'Santorini!'

'You mock me, my child, but He is the one who will judge me!'

'You did not let any of your victims get judged by Him.'

'Didn't I? They came to His house, to me, His representative on Earth. According to His law, they were all sinners that deserved punishment. I ended their wicked ways and send them to him to be judged.'

'Oh, you sound so righteous, don't you? How come you did not get your hands dirty, then? You know, what I believe? You are a lonely, sick-in-the-head, old man that is dying and decided to have some sick fun. You lied and manipulated people that trusted you with their problems.

They came to you for help and all they got was death.' Ioli's voice got louder by the word. Father Avgoustino leaned forward, ready to answer back, but a deep coughing sound muted his words. He spat blood from his mouth and gasped for air. His heart raced into three digit beats and the monitor went crazy.

'Nurse? Nurse?' I shouted.

'Stand back,' she ordered, flying into the room.

'Code Blue,' she yelled, pushing the red button on the wall. In a matter of seconds, more medical staff rushed through the door. The doctor fought to keep him alive.

With a bloody, enigmatic smile, Father Avgoustino left this world.

'May God not have mercy on his soul...' Ioli mumbled and walked out.

Father Avgoustino was not the only one leaving this earth at that very moment. My cell rang as I stood watching the doctor announce the time of death.

'Hello?'

'Costa...'

'Mum? Hey, how you doing ma?'

'Your father...'

Silence.

'Ma?'

'He... He fell asleep and he did not wake up...'

Numbness overtook me and in a zombie-like state, I sat down. A part of my soul shriveled inside and slowly disintegrated. My father, my idol, my hero. Gone. The man who was always there for me. And I was not there for him.

'The funeral is next Wednesday, if you are not too busy for that too.'

'Ma, don't... I...'

'I don't want to hear it. I have to mourn my husband and plan a funeral. Bye.'

So this is what it really feels like when people say *I feel like shit.*

I managed to pull myself up and hauled my body out of the hospital. Ioli followed shortly after. She only had to take one look at me. She ran up to me, the wind twirling dead bronze leaves around her feet.

'What's wrong?'

'Mum called. My father didn't make it.'

'Costa, I'm so sorry. Here, sit down.'

We sat on the nearby metal bench and there in her arms, I cried on her shoulder.

'I should have been there.'

Chapter Thirty-Four

NEW YORK

People die all the time.

Winter is not the time for a burial in New York.

My two thoughts as we exited the Greek Orthodox church after my father's funeral service. Thin snowflakes were dancing around in the strong, icy wind. Visibility was low as the parade of cars made their way up to Saint Michael's cemetery. Black umbrellas exited the vehicles first, black clothed men and women followed. My mother leaned on me as we led the way up to my father's final resting ground. My sisters, cousins, aunts, relatives and family friends walked behind us through the rusty gates and over the yellowing grass. The grass disappearing, getting buried as the snow started to pile up. Scattered tombstones made up the scenery, while naked trees stretched out their creepy tentacles. My mother was never one to hold a grudge, especially at times like this. She was a Greek mother and her only son was her rock at a time like this.

As they lowered down his casket, neither of us could fight back our tears. As I wiped away the falling drops of pain pushing up my dark shades I saw her. There she was, standing amongst the crowd. My ex-wife Tracy. She smiled at me and even under these circumstances, it warmed my heart.

New York
Three years earlier

It had been the perfect family day out.

The Bronx River Festival took place on a warm Saturday in July. My beautiful wife Tracy, our nine year old angel, Gabriella and I were upon 2Train heading to Burke Avenue, west of Bronx Park where the festival was in full swing. Gabriella looked stunningly beautiful for a young girl, in her white Benetton dress and her hair tied up into two ponytails.

'She is as excited as a porcupine meeting a pineapple,' Tracy joked and we all laughed. Gabriella always laughed at her mother's sayings, even though most of the time she had no idea what she was talking about. Why would a porcupine be so happy to meet a pineapple anyway?

The Bronx River Festival was a celebration of the Bronx River with loads of activities on deck for the entire family. Gabriella eagerly looked forward to the nature scavenger hunt where she had high hopes of proving to daddy what a good little investigator she had become. Tracy was going to take part in all the calorie-burning activities like capoiera and power yoga while I was going to stand by a tree smoking in secret so Gabriella would not see me. I would stand there all day if Tracy let me, admiring the two of them and occasionally waving and giving a thumbs-up to every 'Daddy, daddy look.'

The festival did justice to the saying *time flies when you're having fun* and four hours went by without any of us noticing. It was time to head back home.

The party of three came out from the underground holding hands, letting the love flow through us. Little Gaby was ecstatically happy, having played all sorts of games, eaten a bunch of junk food mama would not have allowed on a normal day and she had her face painted as a fairy princess.

The tires of the car racing round the corner and down the street made us jump and as I turned around, I saw the barrels of their guns sticking out from behind the slightly opened tinted windows of a black Lincoln MKS.

'Get down,' I yelled, pushing Tracy to the ground behind a parked yellow Chevrolet and fell upon my baby girl, rolling with her behind a rusty dumpster. The sound of multiple and constant firing penetrated the air and it only took one bullet, out of the one hundred and sixteen bullets fired, to penetrate Gabriella's left lung. Blood started oozing out pretty quick and soon her white dress had turned dark red.

'Long live Sanchez, asshole,' a shrill voice was heard and the car sped away to oblivion.

I knelt and held her close in my arms and that's where little Gabriella 'Gaby' Papacosta left her last breath.

Tracy screamed erratically for help and an ambulance, but I knew it was too late. I closed my baby's eyes and kissed her gently on the forehead. As her heart stopped beating, I felt mine break and all I could do was cry. I held on to Gaby until the paramedics pulled me off, having already given a strong sedative to Tracy, who -curled up behind the Chevrolet's wheel- kept repeating 'no, no... Costa, say it isn't so.'

We did not speak to each other again, not even at the funeral and one fine, sizzling N.Y. August evening, Tracy came out of the master bedroom, suitcases in hand.

'I always hated your job. I told you to accept a desk job, once we had a child. This is all your fault,' she cried with no more tears left in her eyes.

'I know.'

'Bye, Costa.'

And just like that, she left my life. The next week, I boarded a plane set for Greece. A man with nothing to lose. A man ready to take on the most dangerous homicide cases.

New York, Papacosta family home
Present Day

Mother sat numb on her living room sofa. Her apartment filled with people, but she had never felt more alone in her life. The house she shared with the love of her life suddenly felt colder. It was no longer a home. The walls were just walls and all the belongings in it, seemed meaningless. She smiled politely and accepted condolences, each time wanting to scream out that she could not bear to live another second without him.

Tracy came round as well. My mother kissed her and stroked her cheek. Not long ago, the two cried frantically in each other's arms, when fate brought them the loss of their precious Gaby.

'He is in the kitchen,' Maria calmly said to her. I stood

on the kitchen balcony with my childhood best friend Jimmy, having a much-needed smoke and whiskey coke.

'Hey, Jimmy.'

'Tracy! So good to see you.' He kissed her on her cheek and made up a ridiculous excuse to go inside.

'I have played this scene so many times in my head and now I am standing opposite you and I have nothing to say.' It felt so good to hear her voice again. That sweet tone whispering *I love you* in the morning, making everything seem worthwhile. We had our ups and downs, like everybody else, but we weren't strong enough to deal with Gaby's death. We had struggled to get pregnant. Nothing worse for a newlywed couple to find out, than a hostile uterus and a low sperm count. Add in, our hectic lifestyle as a corporate lawyer and a homicide detective and it was a miracle Gaby was ever conceived.

'You've changed your hair.'

She blushed and the corners of her lips moved upwards. Tracy had always been proud of the fact, that I always noticed the little changes she would make. A different shade of dye, a different nail color, a new shirt, a new day cream, a new perfume. Her girlfriends would complain about their partners paying no attention to their efforts and Tracy would joke how they all should marry a detective who notices everything.

My once brunette wife admitted that after I left, she had dyed it black. Now, she glowed under her golden wheat hair.

'I guess, based on the circumstances, I should have left it black. My poor Sebastian. What a great man.'

I looked down in sorrow. 'I was not even here when he died. I left Maria alone to deal with it and now I will never see him again.'

'Oh, Costa...' She opened her arms and I fell into her. Her hand gently caressed my thinning hair.

'Come on,' she finally said. 'Let's go get some food into you. Everyone brought something. I am sure Mrs. Andreou brought stuffed vine leaves.'

'Mmm, koupepia.' I let Tracy pamper me for the evening. I tried hard not to read too much into her smiles and support. My father had just died. Then again, my mind was never one to listen to logic. It wrote the scenario that suited it the best. She was here and she was ready to sort things out. Legally, we were still married. With problems and issues, but married.

The day after, I call her up for coffee.

'Sounds great. There is this new place I love, opened a few months ago.'

And just like that, a tragic accident brought together two estranged people. Two people that let life get the better of them. We talked, we joked, and we held hands. Our second *first date*. She invited me over to see the new place she was renting.

'What a wonderful view,' I said as I gazed upon New York's skyline. Rain hit hard against the window. Tracy lit the fireplace and stood behind me. Her hands circled around me and she kissed the back of my neck. She breathed heavily. 'I have missed you so much, there are no words.'

I turned around and kissed her cherry lips while my hands entered her hair, pulling her close. We stumbled together backwards, items of clothing falling to the floor. We lay naked in front of the fireplace, hands, lips and tongues journeying upon familiar ground. She felt so warm. I slowly entered her and got lost in her green eyes that shined bright, reflecting the flames of the fire. We switched positions with teenage excitement. We wanted everything from each other. To live everything good once again. Desperately filling in the three year gap. With me on my back and Tracy on top of me, I enjoyed her beauty.

'You are as beautiful as the first day I laid eyes on you...'

'Trying cliché compliments with me, mister Papacosta?'

'I...'

'It's working...' she laughed and seconds later, exploded with joy. She fell to my side and I rolled above her. She groaned, feeling me again deep inside her, thrusting away. I could not believe it was happening. A story of fiction, brought to life. Love with Tracy. All my body shivered as I came. Every cell in my body was screaming for her. We stayed in each other's arms, afraid to let go. Night came and found us asleep, hand in hand, leg upon leg. We awoke near midnight, ordered Chinese and watched late night shows. The three year gap vanished into the cold air outside and the cleansing rain washed away sins of the past.

Chapter Thirty-Five

ARIADNE METAXA'S OFFICE

June

'For someone who despises the summer, you sure are in a good mood,' Ariadne joked. She looked younger with her hair pulled back into a high ponytail, slight color decorating her pale skin and a breezy summer dress on.

'You have air-con,' I replied. 'New chair?'

'You like it?'

I sat down into the blue leather armchair. 'Honestly? Not as comfortable. Anyway, I am not one who enjoys change. I'll get used to it.'

'You have had some major changes happen over the last few months. Changes for the better.'

'It still seems unreal that Tracy is here.'

'How is she coping with our crazy society?'

I chuckled. 'She would agree on the crazy part. I believe she's doing fine. Everyone at the company is either a foreigner or uses English at the office, so she has had no linguistic barriers. She likes new challenges and unlike me, she has fallen in love with the weather.'

'They do say we are the world's most beautiful country. Why wouldn't she fall in love? And you? How's your mind dealing with all the joy?'

'Tough to say. You know, better than anyone, the dark place I lived and thrived in. After Gaby, I did not care if I lived or died. I drifted through life waiting to be released.'

'And where is that darkness now?'

'Still lingering around, though over the last year it has shrivelled up quite a bit.'

'Because of Ioli?'

'Well, yeah. She helped me find purpose again at work and now Tracy is back, I feel I have a purpose in life, too.'

'And the conflict between the two lives?'

'Elaborate, please,' I said, leaning forward.

'You have admitted being good at what you do, because you took risks. You hunted the worst kind of killers and sadistic murderers. You loved putting yourself in danger's way. Can you still do that? Knowing that Tracy is at home waiting for you?'

I took a moment. 'I...' I raised my hands. 'I don't know.'

'Changes require us to re-arrange our goals and our priorities, Costa. Solving murder cases is who you are.'

'Ioli says that facing death in our line of work makes her feel alive.'

'Maybe Miss Ioli should also pay me a visit.'

I threw my head back and laughed.

'In a sense that she appreciates life more. Maybe, facing death will make me appreciate having Tracy back in my life and force me to be more careful.'

Who could have known how much death, I was going to witness the following day?

Chapter Thirty-Six

CASE NO.3: THE BLACK HORSE - JUSTICE, LAW GIVER, FAMINE, DESTRUCTIVE POWER OF A CLASS GAP ON A SOCIETY.

Spring came and went rather uneventfully. No major crimes, no mystery deaths. Just some good old, clean-cut cases. The husband *did it* out of jealousy, the boss *did it* for the money, the best friend *did it* out of revenge. I've played Cluedo games more difficult to solve.

Ioli took over most cases, giving me time to reconnect with Tracy, who took the leap and moved to Greece. She took one look at my filthy man-hole of an apartment and the very next day we were searching for real estate. A brand new, two bedroom, ground floor apartment with a small garden sealed the deal.

Ioli spent most of her newly found free time with her hobbies. She cooked and ate, worked out hours at the gym, practiced her shooting at the police range site and painted our office wall cherry red. It promoted creativity she said. The chief ordered it repainted white, but no one bothered changing it. It took a while, but it slowly won the grumpy old man over. She, also, spent hours reading. Every now and then, she would call over a quote.

'She was like the moon, you never saw all of her. Lovely, isn't it?'

I would nod in agreement. The worse came when she read a comedy. She would laugh out loud and shout out just the punch line, leaving out the rest of the funny parts.

'And then she lit the fireplace!' And she would laugh. 'All the money was in there!'

The only thing being killed was time. Until the second day of June.

Summer in Greece. A sentence of joy, of careless holidays, of turquoise waters and of long sandy beaches. For me, a sentence of sweat. Of constant heat waves, strong enough to melt your insides like a spider's poison.

I kept myself busy, by organizing my court dates. I had to testify on the cannibalistic cleaning lady. An elderly woman who kept her dead husband in the freezer and decided to cook and eat him. Ioli typed in the testimonies for me to go over.

The door flew open without a knock. It could only be the chief.

'Costa, Ioli,' he grunted our names. His tender way of a good morning.

'I've got a case for you two.'

'Since when do you come down here personally to deliver cases?'

He smiled at me and threw a photo of a young woman hanging from the ceiling. 'She hanged herself last night or so the local police reported, on Corfu island.'

'So it was murder?' Ioli asked.

'Maybe. Most likely a suicide.'

'Then, how is this...'

He did not let me finish.

He threw another photograph on the table. Another

hanging body. A man in his early thirties. 'Zakynthos. Last night.' He threw another photo. 'Kefalonia. Last night.' Another. 'Paxoi. Last night.' He laid seven photographs before our eyes.

Seven islands.

Seven bodies.

Chapter Thirty-Seven

The Ionian Islands or Eptanisa (Seven Islands) as they are known in Greece are a group of islands scattered along Greece's western coastline. Most were never subjected to Ottoman rule making the islands were a haven for 'men of the spirit'. The arts flourished under Venetian rule and Italian influences can be found in local cuisine, rhythm of language and architect.

Nowadays, they enjoy being featured in travel magazines, Hollywood movies and top ten lists with the world's best beaches.

'Seven people, each on a different island, islands called The Seven Islands, all commit *suicide* on the same day?'

'You think they were murdered?' Ioli asked.

'Maybe. Or at least they are connected. This is one hell of a coincidence, if not.'

'If they were all found this morning, it is likely that they wanted to be found. I mean, if it was planned, a body not being found would ruin the whole design.'

'How do you feel about splitting up?'

'I was thinking the same thing. I thought... as you are shit scared of flying...'

'I am not scared...'

She raised her voice and continued 'You take the speed boat down to Kythira and work yourself upwards while I'll fly to Corfu and work myself down. We will probably meet somewhere in the middle.'

'Sounds like a plan, Cara.'

'By the way, how come it's just the two of us? I thought a team would be sent to each island.'

'The chief said it would look bad to local authorities. Athenian investigators stomping in, taking over their cases. Cases that, at the moment, are classified as suicides. Each island's authority is in charge, until a greater connection is made. We are just assisting. Basically, we will check if they are actually suicides and look for connections between them.'

'Sounds like a plan, as you say.' She got up and touched my shoulder gently. 'Take care.'

'Be careful.'

'Aren't I always?' she laughed, gave me a nudge and walked out the door.

Seven islands. Seven bodies. What a way to kick off your summer.

Chapter Thirty-Eight

ISLAND OF KYTHIRA

By midday, I had docked on the little island of Kythira. The island lies opposite the Peloponnese peninsula, far away from the other six islands, with which it forms the group of the seven islands.

I stood on the wooden dock, my eyes taking in the picturesque town of Chora. The white-painted houses ran down the side of the slope, towered by the tall walls of the castle that occupied the top of the hill. I took a deep breath. A delight to my lungs. The air much purer than the polluted Athenian air. The sandy beach filled with tourists, local and foreign alike.

'Fancy a ride, sir?' a heavyset man with a thick black mustache offered, horse and carriage behind him.

'No, thank you. I believe I am being picked up.' I gazed around the dock. I saw a uniformed constable standing up amongst his friends at a coffee shop opposite the quiet street. He took one last sip and ran over to greet me.

'Constable Stavros Souris,' the dark haired young man

introduced himself with a sincere islander smile. 'This way, Captain,' he said, picking up my small suitcase.

I walked behind him, shades and hat on, avoiding the burning sun. The short man walked tirelessly ahead.

'Erm, Stavro?'

'Yes, sir?'

'Where is your car?'

He smiled. 'No car. Everything is a ten minute walk away. It is just around the corner.' We turned right, walking upon a bricked path that led us through people's back gardens. The flowers that had blossomed during spring were already showing signs of fading away, melting under the summer sun.

A blue-painted wooden door with an X formed by yellow police tape awaited us ahead. A female constable stood by the door. She nodded seriously as Stavro introduced us. Then, she opened the door and under the tape we went. Stavro stopped by the arch that separated the living room from the hall.

'In there,' he said and froze.

I entered the near empty room. A woman's body hung from the ceiling by a thick sailor's rope. The rope was tied from a strong wooden beam that crossed the room. A kitchen chair was knocked to the ground. I wore my gloves and pushed back her black hair from her face.

'Identity?'

'Rita Simonide. Age 37. Rented out the house from the old lady next door around Easter. Kept to herself. She was some sort of writer we were told.'

'Who found her?'

'Mrs. Comninou, the old lady renting the place. She brought her breakfast every morning at seven.'

'Where's the doctor?'

'He is on his way. I texted him as soon as you arrived. He had patients to see. He will be here soon. He lives round the corner.'

'What's this?' I picked up the nylon bag from the worn sofa.

'The suicide note.'

'Difficult it may be, to argue suicide is not a sin
God's soul inside me, in my inner temple in
Only Samson's viewed as good and just
My death, my exit, a necessity, a must,' I read.

'I think you should call your priest too.'

'On it,' the eager-to-help officer replied.

Island of Kerkyra

Ioli had arrived earlier than me in Kerkyra, known around the world as Corfu. Greece's northwestern frontier and home to the Ionian University, where Eftychia Stauropoulou taught religious studies. Until the previous night, when she leapt to her death, her neck tied to her heavy wooden bed. Her lifeless body swung outside her bedroom window, revealed by the birth of dawn.

Ioli stood over the body that had been pulled into the bedroom for obvious reasons. The thirty year old woman had died instantly; the fall breaking her neck, snapping it into pieces. Corfu's coroner explained to Ioli that 'no violent marks were found or any defense wounds' and the local police added 'the house was fully locked from the inside. She was alone.'

'We found this in her bathrobe pocket,' a freckled sergeant said, passing her the suicide note.

'I came naked from my mother's womb and I shall have nothing when I die. The Lord gave me everything I had, and they were His to take away. Blessed be the name of the Lord.'

Underneath she had written three names. Jacob, Job, King David.

Island of Kythira

The doctor in Kythira ruled out foul play and based on the scene, I agreed. The priest shined more light.

'Samson sacrificed himself to save others. The priest said it is the only suicide in the Bible looked upon favorably. For some reason, Rita Simonide felt like she had to die and was trying to justify her decision,' I said to Ioli over the phone.

'Mine quoted the Bible too, from the book of Job. I googled the three names she wrote underneath and I found that all three mentioned, had what we would describe today as depression. Costa, if all seven left a religious suicide note...'

'That's our connection.'

'Another priest brainwashing easy victims?'

'Maybe. Though is there one that travels the islands? Each has their own congregation.'

'Mine wasn't from Corfu. She only taught here.'

'Mine wasn't from here either. I'm going to call Polina back at HQ to see if she has finished with the background checks. Hopefully, she will have their permanent residence.'

'Be careful with your sweet talk around that one, now Tracy is back.'

'Huh?'

'You men are so oblivious. Polina has a crush on you.'

'Ridiculous. I could be her father.'

'*Whose your daddy* is quite a common phrase here in Greece and that is all I'm saying. Anyway, I'm off to Paxos. Just thirty minutes away.'

'It will take me a couple of hours to Zakynthos. I'll call you when I'm done.'

I dialled Polina's number.

'Yes, Captain?'

'Demetriou, are you done with the background checks of...'

'Just finished a case of Captain Germanos and I will be right on...'

'I want it now,' I raised my voice.

'On it right away, Captain,' her voice lost its sweet tone.

'And Demetriou, call my house number in a couple of hours and inform my wife that I will not be returning tonight. I will be too busy to call and I don't want her to worry.'

'Wife, sir?' she asked puzzled.

'Yes, wife. Why do you ask?'

'I was under the impression you were divorced. My mistake.'

'Yes, your mistake. Now, get busy with the checks. I want to know if all victims were visitors to the islands and if so, where was their permanent residence.'

'On it, boss.' And the phone went silent. A feeling of remorse swam over me. I shook it off. It was for the best. Ioli is always right and there was no need in leading the poor girl on.

Ioli and I were each faced with a male body this time.

Island of Zakynthos

My heart skipped a beat as the speed boat passed by Nauagio beach. The famous shipwreck grew out of the sand in the isolated bay. The beach served as one of Tracy's and mine's first honeymoon stops. It had been her first time in Greece and she fell in love with the exotic island.

The speed boat flew by ships busy with unloading thrilled tourists that had waited a lifetime to visit one the landmark beaches of the world. Soon, I had docked in Eptanisa's most populous city, Zakynthos town. A silent sergeant drove me to the third floor apartment where thirty-two year old Demetris Papademetriou, an athlete signed to a local soccer team, ended his life.

He had placed a plastic bag over his head and tied it tightly round his throat. He sat on the balcony, facing Faneromeni church. Another body, another note.

'1 Samuel, 31:3-6,' I read the ripped piece of kitchen roll. 'A bible, please,' I requested.

'One minute, Captain,' the young sergeant replied. He took out his phone. 'There is an app... Wait... Tell me again the verse.'

'1 Samuel, 31:3-6. Read it to me.'

'The fighting grew very fierce around Saul, and the Philistine archers caught up with him and wounded him severely. Saul groaned to his armor bearer: take your sword and kill me before these pagan Philistines come to run me through and taunt and torture me. But his armor bearer was afraid and would not do it. So Saul took his own sword and fell on it. When his armor bearer realized that Saul was dead, he fell on his own sword and died beside the king. So Saul, his three sons, his armor bearer and his troops all died together that same day.'

'That's all of it?'

'Yes, sir.'

'So, the king lost it all and killed himself. What did you lose, Demetri?' I stared into his hollow blue eyes.

***

Island of Paxos

Ioli too was faced with a young man's body. A music teacher, Nikolas Perikli, alone on holiday in the quiet town of Gaios, leapt to his death from his holiday balcony to the hotel's inner garden. He had used metal wire and as he fell, the wire viciously cut into his skin. He died instantly by the snapping of the neck. His body, pulled by gravity, slowly cut away from his head and fell to the ground. The head fell too, rolling along the stone path and into the swimming pool. The morning's cleaning lady who whistled as she swept between the neatly placed sunbathing beds, suffered a severe heart attack at the sight of the floating head.

Ioli spent a good hour, photographing the scene and collecting evidence. She wanted to make sure beheaded Nikola took his own life.

A note slept amongst the dust, left on the glass coffee table that with the old couch, took up most of the living area.

'Judas, heaven or hell? Forgiving father, who can tell?' Ioli read. 'Funny how we all turn poetic at the end,' she whispered.

The female constable smiled uncomfortably at her. 'We've never had such a gruesome crime scene before. Most come here to enjoy the serenity offered.'

'Looks like, this guy needed more peace than was offered.'

She picked up her phone and walked out of the unembellished hotel and into the vast village square. The coffee shops and ice-cream parlors were in full swing, serving sunburned, lobster-colored tourists. She gazed into the deep, blue ocean just feet away and dialed my number. I had just read the note from my scene.

'Costa, another note, another suicide, another person from out of town.'

'Same here. I think these people were burdened with something and resorted to killing themselves as to redeem themselves. I think they must all have been deeply religious.'

'But isn't suicide a sin, according to religion?'

'Maybe that is why they are leaving the notes. Explaining their choice somehow.'

'Has Polina called?'

'No, not yet.'

'I'm thinking maybe some sort of support group. They must have known each other. No way am I believing seven people committed suicide on seven different islands all at the same time. The doctors we have spoken to, place the time of death between midnight and 2 A.M.'

'Also, the way of death intrigues me. Why not put a pistol in your mouth? Or poison? Or get creative with a knife and so on...'

'Exactly. Too many similarities. They knew each other. Polina needs to hurry up with the background checks.' And with that, the tone went dead. Ioli ran and boarded the coast guard's ship, ready to set sail for Lefkada. I, too, wrapped up in Zakynthos and left for Ithaki, Odysseus's famous island. Hours later we both set out for our final island, Kefalonia.

Island of Kefalonia

We met exhausted in Argostoli, Kefalonia's capital town, as the bright summer sun dipped into the horizon and light vanished from the sky. No moon, not even a slice.

'You look like shit.'

'Well, thank you, Miss Sunshine. Now, there's a way to greet your superior officer.'

'Well, excuse me, Captain Papacosta. I promise to behave,' she said, forcing a tired smile. 'My feet are killing me.'

'My back keeps reminding me of my age,' I laughed.

'How was Ithaca?' she asked.

'I went to a small fishing village called Kioni bay. A painter from Athens was renting a small fishing hut. Sixty-seven years old, an Anastasia Pappa. I found her hanging by a fishing rope from the ceiling. The note said that death comes for us all, life given to us will leave our body sooner or later. She wrote a prayer and finished it with Father, here I come. You?'

'Kalamos village in Lefkada. Idalia Rapti, the victim's name. She fits the profile. Out of towner; religious. Moved to the island to join a monastery and become a nun. She was only eighteen. I could not bear to watch her skinny body swinging from the chandelier. So young. Beautiful girl, too. Her note was just one line. I have lived in hell, wherever I go now will be a step up!'

'All these people have a story to be told. All lived in Athens by the way. Polina finished with the background checks. So far, that is their only thing in common. We will visit all of their next of kin and hope to find out more. Let's finish up with our seventh body, go to the hotel Polina booked for us and tomorrow morning I'll be taking the ferry to the mainland and you will fly out at night. You sure you won't be coming with me?'

'I see no point in sitting in a boat for hours and then on a bus for even more hours when I can easily take those big metallic birds that were invented to save you time. It's only an hour's flight! That shrink needs to work on your fears if you ask me,' she joked and laughed.

'I don't mind *big* planes...'

Ioli stopped laughing and gave me a judgmental look.

'Well, I do, but I can still fly in them. It's these tiny little small puny tin boxes that fly the domestic flights. They turn my stomach into jelly and my heart into a racehorse. No, thank you.'

'Whatever you say, Captain. So, who's our next victim?'

'Agatha Richardson. Sixty-two years old, from the UK. She lived and worked in Athens as a book editor for translated works. She retired and moved here five months ago.'

Argostoli town was built in a bay within a bay and boasted some of the calmest waters in Greece. The houses were buried in the green scenery provided by the hills behind it. It looked like the perfect place to retire to. Live in peace the rest of your days. *Get a grip, Costa. You're turning fifty, not eighty.*

After introductions were made with the local police, they led us through an arched doorway that swallowed you into a colorful indoor garden.

'It smells lovely,' I commented. The local police officers exchanged looks.

'Yes... Especially in contrast with inside,' a young, blonde constable mumbled.

I opened the door of the 19th century stone house which stood at the end of a row of red roses. That's when the horrid smell hit us. A mixture of stale foods, blood and animal urine sprinkled with an odor of feces, lingered in the air.

'Go on,' Ioli said.

'You first.'

'Man, woman, cockroach?' I suggested our version of rock, paper, scissors.

'On three. One... two... three.'

The local police stood amazed, watching as I used my index fingers by the side of my head as antennas and Ioli acted as if she was scratching her balls.

'Man beats cockroach,' she proudly declared. 'This way, sir,' she showed me the way.

'In the kitchen. To your left, Captain,' the blonde constable spoke up.

The narrow hallway unfolded in front of us, filled with trays of kitty litter. Nothing had been cleaned for days. Fourteen bowls of different colors were placed side-by-side on the kitchen door. The milk gone bad, smelled nasty. We walked slowly into the kitchen. The round kitchen table housed a large pool of blood. Bloody paw prints were all over the table and tiled white floor. She had provided her cats with one good last drink. Cats with bloody faces, sitting outside the window, frantically meowed to be let back in.

'It took us all day to remove them from the house. That is why we did not leave any windows open to let some fresh air in,' the constable explained.

We hardly heard him. We were both staring up in shock. Agatha Richardson sure did use her imagination with her self-strangling. Maybe she had edited too many thrillers and horror stories. She had tied her wrists, ankles and neck with barbed wire. She passed the barbed wire round the kitchen's two thick, cherry wood beams and connected the wire to her motorized garden hose collector. She, then, turned the machine on and it slowly gathered the barbed wire, twisting it round and round. It had no trouble, lifting the light-weight, fragile lady to the beams. The wire pierced through her skin and strangled her neck, cutting through her carotid artery. Warm blood sprang into the air, spaying the kitchen red and provided a fountain of fresh blood for her feline friends.

'Where's the note?' Ioli asked.

'Sin by sin, they gather, pray by pray, they fade... no more light for me, I linger in the shade...' I read the bagged piece of pink paper passed to me by the local police.

'She sounds tormented. What I don't get is even if they, religious as they seem, could get past the fact that religion views suicide as a sin, why did they feel like God would not forgive them? She wrote *Sin by sin, they gather, pray by pray, they fade... no more light for me, I linger in the shade...* She understood that with prayer her sins faded. So why kill yourself? And the way she chose? She wanted to feel pain. She believed she deserved pain.'

'I'm lost for words,' I answered honestly, puzzled by the case.

'Well, that's a first.'

We examined evidence collected by the local authorities and discussed the case with the town's only coroner. Another suicide by all means.

All seven people dead by their own hand, by their own free will.

I looked at my watch. Ten at night. 'I feel drained of energy.'

'Room service and sleep?'

'I feel like a gyro.'

'You and your junk food.' She rolled her eyes. 'You're the boss. Let's grab a bite and head on over to our hotel.'

An hour later, we were both feeling better. Two kebabs, fries and a couple of ice-cold beers journeyed down to my empty stomach. What helped more, was the environment. We sat in the main square, tourist watching as we ate. The well-lit stone square featured everything a visitor could ask for. Souvenir shops, restaurants and ice-cream parlors surrounded it. We watched their happy, relaxed faces. Their hand-in-hand, moon-lit strolls. Their carefree aura.

Their happiness felt contagious. I envied them and let my mind drift to a daydream where Tracy and I would go on vacation together. In love again.

Ioli guiltily enjoyed our street food and in a sleepy state of mind, she closed her eyes and drifted off to dreamland.

'Lovely place...' I started to say. 'Oh, sorry. I did not realize...' I lowered my voice.

She waved her hand to signal not to stress. 'Let's go get some shut eye.'

Our family-run hotel stood at a distance of a five minute walk. Much-needed minutes for our food to go down.

We checked in with the jovial receptionist and took the keys to our rooms. Within ten minutes, we had showered, undressed and fallen fast asleep. For the first time in a long time, Ioli enjoyed an eight hour slumber.

I, on the other hand, was once again tormented by my nightmares.

'Thank you for all my new friends, daddy,' Gaby sang happily. She swung on a swing set built out of corpses. Agatha and Rita were the legs, Idalia and Anastasia were the top beam, while Demetris, headless Nikola and Eftychia formed the swing.

'Let's play ball,' she screamed, throwing me Nikola's head and waking me up in a cold sweat.

Chapter Thirty-Nine

A hot day followed the hot sticky night. The summer was welcoming its first of many heat waves. A huge red ball of fire sneaked out of the sea and climbed up into the sky. By ten o'clock it felt difficult to move, let alone think.

Ioli and I exited the air conditioned breakfast room and said our goodbyes. I rushed to catch the ferry, while Ioli had hours to kill until her flight to Athens.

'Even though my mood is not the greatest, I can't miss such an opportunity. I've always wanted to visit Myrtos beach.'

'Myrtos beach?'

'You've never heard of it?'

She watched, amazed, as I shook my head that I had not.

'One of the best beaches in Greece.' She took out her phone, fiddled around for a second or two and raised it up to my eyes.

'It looks beautiful. I'm happy you're taking some time for yourself. You're too young to get sucked in by all this.'

'Don't start, grandpa,' she giggled.

'I'm just saying.' And with that, I set off for the port.

Ioli returned to her room to change. She undressed and put on her blue bikini. She stood in front of the mirror and forced a smile. Time had started to take its toll on her body. For the time being, it was noticeable only to herself. She could see the difference. She always kept fit and did her best to eat healthily. Sometimes, she wondered why. She lived alone, she did not wish for children and after her previous disastrous relationships she did not care much for men either.

'You do it for *you*,' she pumped herself up. 'And you need some color, girl!'

She gathered her shiny black hair into a high ponytail, wore her designer sunglasses and pulled down a short, turquoise beach dress. She picked up a hotel towel and her sunscreen and with an air of relaxation caressing her, she left the hotel for a much-deserved, half-day off. She approached the first taxi from the line of cabs outside and bargained for a *local* price for her day trip.

A breathtaking view awaited her.

She ignored the driver's moaning about the air-conditioning going to waste and opened her window. The fresh air from the mountain road filled the green Mercedes. Down below, miles of unspoiled beaches stretched all the way to the oceanic horizon. Minutes later, the car entered the small village of Divarata. Locals marched up and down, busy setting up their souvenir shops, tavernas and ice-cream parlors. Soon, tourists would flock to their village which stood high above Myrtos Beach. A long winding hair-pin dirt road led down to the white pebble beach. A stretch of round, white cobblestones lay between two of the island's tallest mountains, Agia Dynati and Kalon Oros.

She paid the grumbling driver and took out her camera.

'The most dramatic beach in Greece,' she read from a sign. 'I have had enough drama, thank you,' she joked and photographed the wooden sign.

A well-tanned boy approached.

'Bed and umbrella, five Euros.'

'Great. Here you go,' she said, passing him the note. She laid her soft towel down and fell onto the blue, plastic beach bed.

'Heaven,' she whispered.

She drifted away to the sound of the waves; waves gently crashing against the coastline. She emptied her mind from her worries, filled up her inner energy batteries and got up to cover herself with lotion. She gave her skin ten minutes to soak up part of the lotion and strolled towards the sea.

The crystal clear waters welcomed her. The cool water lured her in. She swam amongst tourists of all ages and nationalities. She enjoyed *people watching*, playing her own little game show, guessing their age, occupation and country of origin.

She swam carefree towards the shore. She stood up, recovered her balance on the sea's sandy floor before exiting and walking clumsily over the sun-caressed hot pebbles. She bought an ice cold lemonade from an old man wearing a heavy thick mustache and a T-shirt with the logo "sexy juices for sexy ladies".

The midday sun roamed the clear sky, burning everything below it. Ioli opened her beach umbrella and hid in the shade that covered her entire bed. She finished off her lemonade, regretted not bringing a book with her and sank into the soft, smooth sunbed.

Hectic screaming made her jump.

She sat up, looking around. People were staring towards a brunette lady leaned over a young boy. Ioli saw the red blood glisten under the Mediterranean sun. She ran over to help the distraught woman. And just like everyone else, she stopped in shock.

Two round holes, one on each hand, pierced through the boy's skin. Same with his feet. A scent of flowers filled the air.

'Stigmata!' an old gypsy lady, selling handmade jewelry out of a scratched wooden box, declared with a shout.

Chapter Forty

CASE NO.4: THE PALE, ASHEN HORSE - DEATH

Sophia stood in front of her bathroom's large, oval mirror. She looked ten years older than she really was. Thirty-six and too many worry lines. Her eyes reflected the dying glow in her soul. She hated feeling tired and drained of energy all the time. Between her two jobs, church and her seven-year-old angel, time was scarce. A widow at thirty-two, she struggled to maintain her household, raise her child and keep her faith in a God who deemed part of his mysterious plan to have the love of her life, Father Kypriano, die of pancreatic cancer. A tragic loss of a much loved priest.

Her small community offered to help out financially, but she would hear no word of it. She worked the morning shift at Mister Kyro's bakery and spent her evenings sewing and altering clothes. She'd always had a love for clothes. Not that it mattered anymore. Only black covered her body. She would mourn her husband until the day she died.

Exhausted, at night, she always made time for her little Antony. They played, talked, ate and then her favorite moment of the day came. She read from the Bible to her tucked-in boy. And not just the well-known stories and the moral teaching fables, Sophia read the entire book to him.

Sophia took great pride in noticing how well-behaved her son was. Good-hearted, kind, caring and wise beyond his years. She often joked that he was her 'little saint'.

Lately, she worried about him.

Lately, he would carry around his father's small, wooden crucifix and his Bible never left his school bag.

Lately, a shadow followed him around. He looked distant, lost in thought.

She decided to take him to the beach. Let him live wild and free like boys his age should. After all, it was summer and he should be having fun. An hour later, he fell bleeding in her shaking arms.

'Stigmata,' a filthy-looking woman screamed.

Yes, God did work in mysterious ways.

Chapter Forty-One

Ioli got over her initial shock quicker than most bystanders. She fell to her knees, next to the boy who was desperately gasping for air. His constant screams as a result of the intense, piercing pain prevented the air from traveling to his lungs. He turned red and went into shock.

Then, all of a sudden, his body relaxed. He stretched out his arm and grabbed Ioli's hand. He stared straight into her eyes. The sand swirled around them, pushed off the pebbles by the light breeze.

'Save me,' he whispered. 'Only you can save me,' he continued with his voice trembling.

'Try to relax. Breathe slowly,' she advised as she examined his wounds. You could see right through his hands. She looked down. His feet were also decorated with round, bloody scars.

'Everybody back, please,' a brawny paramedic loudly called out. The crowd moved as one. Everyone stepped back together, giving space to the professionals. Ioli stood up, gently placing her hand on the mother's shoulder. The woman had not stopped wailing since her cry for help.

Soon, Ioli stood alone, watching the howling vehicle carrying the sobbing mother and her poor offspring to the hospital. The crowd had gone back to enjoying the beach, richer with a tale that would be retold by them countless times, each time becoming more exaggerated.

Ioli did not feel like relaxing.

The boy's violet eyes, a la Elizabeth Taylor, lingered in her mind.

She walked all the way up to the village. She paused and enjoyed the magnificent view one last time, before running over to the first cab and ordering the drive to step on it.

The sight of her hotel offered no comfort to her racing heart. She felt strange being so upset. She rushed to her room, undressed in a hurry, took a quick shower and got dressed.

In a matter of minutes, she was once again in the back of a taxi.

'Hospital, please.'

Argostoli's hospital encompassed a group of modern buildings built around the old premises. Some tasteless architect had the idea of painting every other wall red. Ioli rushed between two yellow ambulances and in through the main glassed door.

The emergency room was vacant. A quiet hospital in a quiet town. Its regular customers -old folk with multiple pill prescriptions- entered from the side entrance that led to the pharmacy and appointment desk.

Ioli paced up to the reception. A nurse sat there, busy chatting on the phone to a girlfriend with boss-related problems. She was stunningly beautiful with her curly hair, a rich shade of mahogany, her full cherry lips beneath her high cheekbones and her eyes a dark emerald green.

'One minute, Toula,' she told her friend to wait. 'Yes?'

'A boy was brought in half an hour ago with wounds on his hands and legs...'

'And you are?'

'His aunt,' she lied.

'Room 2-1-2. The doctors are with him. You can wait outside with your sister. She is in a real state.' She smiled politely.

Ioli stormed off and the nurse went back to hearing how Toula had once again been overlooked for promotion.

Ioli pushed the call button and tapped her right foot as she waited for the flickering light to confirm the elevator's movement from the 5th floor on its journey down to her. The elevator doors finally opened, unleashing an unpleasant smell of cheap bleach. One of the few smells Ioli could not stand.

Ioli opted for the stairs, cursing about the seconds lost. The wooden door creaked as she pushed it aside and sprinted up the stairs. She exited onto the second floor corridor, in front of door 202. She looked down the corridor. The brunette from the beach was pacing outside the door; behind which doctors cared for her son.

Ioli hesitated for a minute, took a deep breath and walked over.

'Excuse me, Mrs?'

Red shot eyes turned to see her.

'I am Ioli Cara. I am with the Hellenic Police...'

The woman took a step back. 'The police? Why are *you* here?'

'Oh, I'm not here as a police officer. I was at the beach when the...' She searched for the right word. 'When the incident happened. I just wanted to make sure your son was okay.'

The woman's facial muscles relaxed.

'That's nice of you. No one is telling me anything. I'm his mother, I should be in there with him. He must be so scared right now.' She covered her mouth, sat back down in one of the cold rusty chairs and cried.

Ioli sat beside her, her hand gently comforting the woman.

'I'm sure they will be out any moment now with good news.'

The woman extended her hand and laid it above Ioli's. Through her running tears, she forced a sincere smile.

'Is there anyone I could call, Mrs...?'

'Call me Sophia. No, don't call anyone.'

'Your husband? Mother? It helps to have...'

'Both dead,' Sophia bluntly replied. 'But, you're here,' she continued. 'God always sends the right person.'

'I don't know about that,' Ioli started to say and paused, having noticed a lanky doctor towering them.

'Mrs. Antoniou, I am doctor Papadopoulos.' He read her expression; an expression witnessed in every mother's face. She was ready to interrupt him. He rushed and added 'your boy is fine.'

'Oh, praise the Lord! He is okay!' She squeezed Ioli's hand. 'Can I see him now?'

'He is resting. The ordeal has worn him down. The poor little lad is exhausted. Give him some time. We have cleaned and closed his wounds. May I ask how did he get them?' the doctor asked rather casually. He always tried to sound indifferent. Parents did not take kindly to being accused of hurting or neglecting their children.

'I wish I knew,' Sophia answered softly.

Twenty minutes later, the blinds of the indoor window in room 212 were lifted by a tired looking nurse. Sophia rushed to look through the window. Her Antony looked peaceful. His hands and legs were wrapped in white bandage. She touched the glass window and looked at the floor.

It was in that position that Father Kyriako found her, followed by four reporters, an elderly man wearing a crying-for-an-iron security uniform and the beautiful nurse from the reception.

'You cannot be here. I am calling the police,' the stunning girl shouted.

'Out now,' the security man said with no power in his voice.

Sophia turned her head slightly towards the direction of the commotion. She took out a black headscarf and covered herself. She turned towards the priest.

'Father...' The only word she managed to say before breaking down in tears. The young priest brought her tenderly to his shoulder.

'There, there. Relax.'

The reporters clicked away. Flashes of light bounce around the narrow corridor. Questions followed.

'Is it stigmata?' one of them finally asked.

'Hey! Give the woman some privacy. You heard the security guard. Get out,' Ioli stood up and walked towards the reporters who took an unsure step back.

The security guard smiled at her, but his smile quickly faded as he witnessed the disapproving look of the doctor.

'He just hurt himself playing down at the beach. That's all. Please go, my boy is sleeping and...' Sophia seemed to lose her balance. She wobbled from side to side and fell into the priest's arms. Blood appeared to be running down her covered forehead. Rivers of blood snaked down her porce-lain skin. Father Kyriako pulled off her scarf. Deep scars graced her forehead. More shocking, they formed a pattern. Two lines of dotted scars.

Two nurses rushed to her while the doctor wheeled a bed towards them. Two of the reporters froze, while the others kept on taking photographs. The police, called in by the girl at the reception, arrived to escort the reporters off the premises while the hospital personnel took Sophia away. Ioli was left with Father Kyriako whose hands were shaking. He sat down and prayed. Ioli waited patiently.

'You're a friend of Sophia's?' he finally asked her.

'I was at the beach. Thought I could offer my help.'

He smiled warmly at her.

'Father, if you don't mind me asking. I have heard of stigmata before, mostly in horror movies...'

He waved his hand. 'Junk words by junk reporters.'

'You can say that after what just happened? The boy has marks from the crucifixion and now his mother bleeds from her head... where Jesus wore his thorny crown. I might not be a regular church-goer, but all this,' she waved her hands around 'is not normal.'

'The church does not *officially* recognize stigmata...'

'Just saying the word officially like that, makes me believe that unofficially it does.'

'There have been quite a few cases over the years. Some explained, some not. But, the bottom line is, the press is going to have a field day and I will not allow that to happen to poor Sophia and Antony. They have been through enough.'

Chapter Forty-Two

ATHENS

The following morning, I awoke next to Tracy's warm body. My right leg tangled between hers, my arm wrapped around her. The bed sheet kicked to the floor by two naked lovers; every cell of our body, enjoying the cool chilling air provided by the air conditioning unit. The sun's first rays were sneaking in through behind my thin peach curtain and were dancing around the room. I stared at the mean old clock standing guard on my bedside table. Many fights were fought between me and my morning arch enemy. My nemesis always won.

With great satisfaction, I realized that I had awoken two whole minutes before its menacing eruption. I slowly pulled away from Tracy. She grunted gently and rolled to *her side* of the bed. I stood up naked and hit the turn-off button on my alarm. I stretched, I scratched and I peed. Every man's first ritual of the day.

I tiptoed to the kitchen to prepare a surprise morning coffee for my wife. I smiled reminiscing the previous night. The years apart had made us stronger. We talked like best friends, romanced as newlyweds and screwed like teenagers in a world with no tomorrow. Maybe the late forties were the new late twenties or some bull like that.

'Baby? Baby, wake up. It's seven.'

'Five more minutes,' she managed to say. It was always five more minutes with Tracy.

'I've got coffee!' Now, that caught her attention. She struggled to rise and sit up straight. Her hand asked for its mug. Soon, the hot beverage ran down our throats and the caffeine swam to our brains.

'Another hot day. I should be off. Got seven families to visit today and Ioli hasn't called me back yet. I hope she arrived well last night. Are you going to take the metro to work or do you want me to...'

More awake due to coffee, she placed a full-lip kiss on my talking mouth.

'Mmm, yep, that shut you up. It's too early to talk,' she said and giggled. 'I'll take the metro,' she added after another couple of sips. 'You look all shiny and new. Had a good night's sleep?'

'I wake up like this because of you. You are my life's detergent.'

She managed a sleepy laughter that ended in a yawn. 'You do come up with the weirdest crap when you're trying to be romantic.'

'At least, I try.'

'And succeed,' she replied and placed another kiss on my lips.

'Are you happy here, baby?' I asked.

'Of course, I have you.'

'And you don't miss anything from back home?'

'I miss my therapist.'

Now, it was my turn to laugh.

'Don't laugh. I'm serious. Susan helped me a great deal with... through it all.' Tracy avoided mentioning Gaby. 'And we became great friends, she was a joy to open up to.'

'Why don't you pay Ariadne a visit?'

'You think that would be wise?'

'Why not? It's not like she is allowed to talk about me.'

'Yes, because that is all I talk about!' she said, then got up and ran to the bathroom.

The sound of running water echoed through the room. Steam escaped from below the door. I never understood how this woman could have a hot steamy shower in one of the hottest countries in the world. In the summer, too. I shower with cold water, all year round. And with that last thought, I got dressed, shouted a goodbye and was on my way.

The concrete jungle of Athens sizzled under the huge fireball in the sky. And it was still morning. At least, my car's steering wheel was cool enough to be handled. I took out my notebook and read the names of the seven *victims* and their next of kin, and set off for a long day.

The first of many red lights brought me to a halt. I dialed Ioli's number; still no answer. That is when I noticed the tiny envelope flashing in the top right corner of the screen.

'Costa, I won't be catching my flight out. Long story. I am fine. I will fly out as soon as I've handled a situation that came up here. Sorry, for leaving you alone on such a day. I'll call when I can and explain,' I read and was both puzzled and intrigued. *What was this girl up to, now?*

Absent minded, I turned left onto a one way street, from the exit end. A white delivery van screeched before me. I slammed on the brakes. The two tire-burning vehicles stopped inches from each other.

'I'm so sorry,' I shouted to the angry driver. 'My bad,' I continued and reversed. He honked as he drove slowly past me and flipped me the finger.

The case file had fallen from the seat. Photographs from the scenes had scattered around. I parked to the side and picked them up. Agatha, Rita, Idalia, Anastasia, Demetris, Nikolas and Eftychia all stared at me. All with a story to be told.

Demetris lived with his younger sister, Louiza, in a two bedroom apartment in the prestigious area of Kolonaki, in the heart of Athens. I had decided to start interviewing those closest to me and work my way to the outskirts of Athens.

I drove around the park opposite the modern, cement-colored apartment block. Kids were busy being kids. A football was being kicked around, swings were swinging and slides welcomed bottoms with laughing heads. *If only I was still a father...*

I squeezed my car between an old Honda and an over-flowing trash can. I opened my door, saddened to say goodbye to my air-con. The heat surrounded me, choking me, mocking every dry pore on me. I slammed the car door shut, scaring away rough-looking cats feasting on thrown-out fish bones.

I pushed the button labelled Papademetriou. A soft voice came out of the built-in speaker.

'Yes?'

'Captain Papacosta with the Hellenic Police. I called you yesterday?'

'Yes, of course. Come up, fifth floor, apartment two,' she said, buzzing me in.

I pushed the door open and proceeded towards the elevator that awaited me with open doors. I entered and pressed five. The elevator doors closed, leaving me alone with my reflection. Getting old sucks. Don't let anyone fool you and tell you otherwise. I was getting fatter, with less hair than before and with deep lines decorating my once youthful round face.

I stepped out onto the fifth floor. A row of grey iron doors stood before me. One slightly opened.

'Miss Louiza?' I called through the gap.

'Come in, Captain. Close the door.'

A cool breeze welcomed me in. The living room was vast with a panoramic view of the city.

'Sit down, I'll be with you in a minute,' the voice continued from inside the kitchen. I sat down on the beige leather couch and waited.

A tall brunette appeared through the doorway, silver tray in hand.

'I took the liberty of making you coffee.' She placed the redolent coffee, a glass of iced water and a plate of cinnamon cookies on the cherry wood coffee table.

She wore black and looked sickly pale. She sat down in a huge armchair opposite me. Its size made her look like a child.

'I am sorry for your loss.'

She smiled for a brief second out of politeness and then let her lips drop back to a flat line. I took a sip from my boiling hot Greek coffee.

'Your coffee is exquisite.'

'It's a special kind of coffee. Demetri is a... was a coffee junkie.'

'Nice place. How long have you lived here?'

'Demetri bought this place when he first came to Athens six years ago with big dreams of making it in one of the league's top football clubs. I moved in a year ago. I decided to further my education with a PhD in Literature.'

'Must have cost an arm and a leg. A place like this.' Demetris's background check reported that he was from a poor family living off the land in the agricultural village of Chrisavgi.

She sat up, uneasy.

'He did not manage to pay it off. The bank owns it now. I'll be gone by the end of the month.'

Samuel 31:3-6. Saul lost it all.

'What else did your brother lose?'

'It has been a rough year for Demetri. He lost a lot of his money on investments gone bad, his contract with his club was not renewed, he owed this place and his Maserati and to top things off, his skank of a girlfriend left him for his best friend when they both realized he was a sinking ship. They enjoyed living his lifestyle.' She struggled with her words. Tears of anger were forming in her eyes. 'I tried to help him. I really did. He never did listen to me. He never listened to anybody. I even sought professional help for him as his depression grew. I tried to send him on a couple of blind dates with friends of mine, but it was too late. He was in a very dark place.'

Demetri wasn't the only one in a dark place.

Rita Simonide's husband praised the Lord I had arrived. Murder flashed in his eyes. He paced up and down their living room as he told me their story.

'... Rita was a good woman...' he wept. 'And an excellent mother, a wonderful person...'

'Mr. Simonide, if you could please just take a minute and relax...'

'Relax? Relax! After what they did to my poor Rita?'

'Who did what?' I raised my voice.

He suddenly stopped and sat down on the floor in front of me. He fixed his gaze on the floor and struggled with the words.

'Now, she is dead, I need no revenge, I need no justice. Promise me, you will not take this any further.'

'Mr Simonide, if a crime took place, I am obliged to...'

'Then we have nothing to say here.'

'Did Rita commit a crime?'

'Never.'

'You?'

'No...' He bit his lips. 'Rita was...' He swallowed and exhaled. 'She was raped.'

My eyes grew larger. 'Raped? When?'

'Last month. She was leaving her Christian Ladies group and was ambushed by two men. She fought to...' Tears flowed down and choked his words. 'I wanted to call the police, I wanted to go out and find them myself, but Rita would have none of it. She was such a devout Christian. She said she forgave them and she did not wish everyone, especially our two kids and her mother, to know. But, it did not end there. A few days after the attack, we received a DVD and a letter in a brown envelope, left on our doorstep. It was the worse day of my life. Are you married, Captain?'

I nearly answered *seperated*. 'Yes.'

'Imagine watching your wife being raped. Forced to do unholy things. Two beasts all over her.' He went silent in disgust.

'The letter? What did it say?' I asked, trying to draw his mind away from the images engraved in his mind.

'They wanted 200,000 Euro delivered in a month. Details would follow.'

I looked around. A plain, three-bedroom house, worn

furniture and decorated cheaply. Outside an old Ford. Achillea Simonide worked as a plumber.

'I know what you're thinking,' he chuckled. 'We don't look like millionaires, do we now?'

'I must admit that I was wondering why they would be asking for such a large amount of money from a middle-class family.'

'Rita was a writer. She wrote Christian stories about love, faith and the good in mankind. Her books made over 50,000 per month in sales. She gave most of it to charities. She was actively involved in many support groups for abused children, single mothers and so on. She said the Lord gave her the stories so any profits from them were not hers. She only kept enough to make ends meet and banked a few thousand every month for the kids' studies. She was more concerned about embarrassing her family when the video went public. She said that no one could guarantee that they would not keep coming back for more.'

'Achillea, whoever did this knew the kind of money she was making. Don't you suspect anyone?'

He shook his head. 'Anyway, Rita's wish was to leave things untouched. I respect that and I, too, do not want my children finding out. They have just lost their mother.'

'How about I ask a few questions and see what I can do? Unofficially? And report only to you if I hear anything?'

'No need.'

I did not tell him that I wanted to and had to report it. But, I would make sure nothing got out to the public.

By nightfall, seven stories unfolded before me. Seven tragedies that led seven people to their grave. Demetri lost it all, Rita killed herself to save her family from embarrass-ment, Eftychia was diagnosed with severe manic depression and believed her life was just a test, Nikolas like a second

Judas betrayed his own father and testified against his family's law firm -both his parents were sentenced for money laundering, Anastasia was diagnosed with terminal cancer and had two more painful months to live and Agatha was tormented by her desires. Her computer hard drive was filled with child pornography.

Idalia's story was made known through the morning papers. She had sent in proof to police headquarters before taking her own short life. She was left an orphan at the tender age of twelve and sent to live with her mother's cousin. A cousin who with her scumbag boyfriend, rented little and beautiful Idalia out to older men for a hefty price. Both were arrested, along with a group of sick, perverted *clients*.

God, sometimes you really make me lose all faith in you...

Chapter Forty-Three

DR. ARIADNE METAXA'S OFFICE

Tracy twisted and turned in 'my' armchair. She played with her fingers and avoided eye contact with Ariadne. She had already regretted her decision to come. She remembered how it had taken her months to trust Susan (her previous therapist) with her deepest thoughts and emotions.

'It's our first session. Try to think about it as a visit to a new neighbor. We can talk about the weather, everyday life, fashion...' Ariadne said, reading Tracy's mind.

'Fashion?'

'Athens has nothing to envy from other cities. But, then again, you are a New Yorker.' Ariadne's warm smile lifted Tracy's spirits.

'I must admit, I still haven't learned my ways around the market yet.'

'How about every time you visit me, I let you in on an amazing boutique?'

'I don't know about your professional skills, but you are one hell of a marketing guru.'

'Anything else I can bribe you with?'

'Now that you mention it, I am looking for a better beauty salon.'

Both women shared a laugh.

Ariadne kept the conversation on a friendly note. She always took this as a first approach. Used to traumatized police officers, she knew people needed time to talk about their deepest pains.

Chapter Forty-Four

Ioli awoke before the sun had risen. She sat up and exhaled deeply. The dilemma of staying or leaving kept her awake until midnight. She had to speak to the boy. She had to ask him what he meant. She had to make sure he was going to be better. She knew she was probably reading too much into what he said.

Only you can save me. He would have said the same to anyone standing next to him, right? she thought.

She decided on a cold shower and an ice-cold frappe. It felt good to shower without a rush. Ioli always struggled to be punctual. She worked long hours without slacking off and she would not allow anyone to have something to hold against her. The chief frowned upon officers being late and she never wanted to be at the receiving end of that frown. For her, to be on time meant forcing herself out of bed and running like a headless hen to be on time. Now, she let the water run down her body. She stood there for a while, clearing her mind. She brought the shower gel to her nose. Some sort of Hawaiian tropical flower mixed with honey and milk. The gel turned into foam as she rubbed it gently on her skin. This was not a shower, it was a ritual. She stepped out and naked as she was, she plucked her eyebrows and applied her subtle makeup. Her long black hair was pulled up into a high ponytail. She pulled on her tight blue jeans and a casual white blouse with a discreet v neck.

The frappe mixer soared to life and sun rays sneaked into the room. She pulled back the heavy curtains and exited onto the tiny balcony. The sea's fresh air rushed down into her lungs and Ioli thanked God for Greece's stunning views. The Greek land always running to meet the sea. The clear skies above the turquoise tranquil waters. More divine was the coffee that flowed down her esophagus and into her nervous system. The breakfast buffet did not open for another half an hour, so she settled herself down in a white plastic chair and placed her long legs upon the round balcony table. Her romance novel rose to eye level and Ioli truly let her mind relax.

A flock of noisy seagulls shattered the fantasy world into which she had ventured. As her senses returned to planet earth, she inhaled a whiff of crispy fried bacon.

She was second to the breakfast buffet, beaten by a loud German and his even louder family. By the time Ioli had filled her tray with all sorts of morning goodness -and of course another coffee- the dining room and its balcony were filled with European tourists.

Ioli enjoyed her meal, feeling rather lonely. She people-watched for a while; letting her food settle down and with one last sip of her coffee, she was off to the hospital.

Ioli was the youngest person on the first bus of the morning. The usual group of senior citizens was heading to the hospital to stock up on their medicine. The bus driver smiled warmly at her hopping on and stared through his overhead mirror at the out-of-towner who took a seat in the back. The old bus roared to life and with a screech and a bang, it set off for the hospital. Outside, the small town awoke slowly. Ioli squinted at the sun sneaking up from behind houses with windows and doors still shut.

The bus driver, who was missing a neck and half a brain, drove the entire bendy road with one hand on the wheel. The other was preoccupied with cursing other drivers, talking on the phone, drinking an iced coffee and smoking. The elderly women, accustomed to his driving, exchanged yesterday's news while older men either continued their sleep or argued about politics. All of them oblivious to the chaos unfolding before Ioli's eyes. The driver ran a red light, climbed up and down a pavement, nearly left a row of cars without their wing mirrors, honked cars out of its way and sped down narrow village dirt roads. As the menacing bus slowed to a standstill, she thanked God for sparing her life. She did not thank him as much when she found out from yesterday's beautiful nurse that the Antoniou family were no longer at the hospital. The nurse's jaw dropped upon hearing the profanities Ioli's mouth was capable of.

'What do you mean they left?'

'Mrs. Antoniou checked herself and her boy out, against doctor's orders. We cannot force people to stay.'

'Can you call me a taxi then?' Ioli asked disappointed.

'Sure thing,' the girl smiled in an attempt to cheer her up.

Ioli walked over to a huge vending machine offering a large selection of hot and cold beverages. Most options were covered by a white sticker declaring 'NOT AVAILABLE AT THE MOMENT'. Thankfully, double espresso had no such sticker. She slipped the money into the slot and placed the thick paper cup under the machine's outlet beak.

'It will be here in five.'

'Thank you,' Ioli responded and coffee in hand, she walked outside. A crying for a re-paint bench welcomed her. She kept herself busy by scratching the sun-blistered paint and enjoying her coffee. By the last sip, her carriage had arrived.

'Where to?'

She was ready to name her hotel, when she thought *what the heck? Why not? It's worth a shot.*

'Do you know Sophia Antoniou's residence? I have something for her. I thought she would be here and...'

'Oh, the priest's widow. Yeah, I'll have you there in ten minutes,' he said and did not bother to ask any further questions. He turned up the radio playing the morning news and drove in silence. Ioli's mind wandered and soon she was having an inner discussion about the ups and downs of small societies.

'Just around the corner, ma'am. It is... What the...?'

Around the corner, in contrast to the quiet streets that they had travelled, dozens of people were gathered around news-outlet mini vans. Yellow police tape, stretched across the front yard of the house next to the Antoniou residence, was dancing in the light morning wind. In the driveway, a muted ambulance with its red lights glowing, and two police cars were parked. Cameras were rolling and focused on Sophia. Ioli quickly paid the driver and shot out of the car. She ran over and was relieved to see little Antony, standing all shy behind his mother.

'Mrs. Antoniou, you are saying you saw Saint Gerasimos last night?' a reporter asked with disbelief.

'As real as I see you and you are seeing me, mister. He

came to me and told me that everything will be alright and that the pain will be shared amongst the righteous.'

'Did you see him go next door?'

'No. I was in shock to see my husband following Saint Gerasimo, bless his name!'

The questions kept on coming and Sophia stood her ground.

'Hey kid, show us your hands.' one tall, blonde reporter yelled.

'Hey! This is no sideshow!' Ioli could not restrain her anger. She pushed herself through the pack of wolves and with her arm around the boy she led him inside the house. Sophia was taken aback and took a few seconds to realize that it was the lady from the hospital, just the previous day. She took in a small breath and continued with last night's events.

'Thank you,' Antony said with a strained voice.

'What happened next door?' Ioli stooped to his eye level.

'Elisabeth, the girl next door, woke up with stigmata too.'

Her eyes opened wide. 'You don't say. Like yours?'

'Just her hands. But her wounds weren't all the way through. They did not let me see her. She is a year younger than me and I know I shouldn't be playing with girls, but Elisabeth is pretty cool. And mother likes her too. She is in my Sunday school.'

'Antony... At the beach, do you remember what you said to me?'

The boy nodded. 'I said you would save me and so far you have. I don't like reporters. All they do is talk and talk and ask and ask, but they don't care. Not a single word they say to you is polite or nice. Rude. That's the word Miss Despo would use.'

'Who?'

'Miss Despo, my teacher.'

She looked straight into his peculiar violet eyes. 'Save you from what?'

The door being flung open, startled them.

'How dare you?' Sophia asked, closing the door behind her.

'I...'

'No, no. You don't get to speak to me. Who told you, you could take my boy away?'

'Sophia, I apologize, but it was no place for him out there.'

'That is for his mother to decide. His marks are for the world to see. They are not his to own. Neither are mine. Jesus Christ, our Lord and Savior, gave them to us for a reason. And now, Elisabeth next door? All this means something.'

'I respect your beliefs, Sophia. I acted on impulse. Antony looked so uncomfortable out there. I'm sorry. I only wanted to help.'

'This is all too much for me...' Sophia leaned back against the wall and slid down to the tiled floor. Tears formed around her eyes' black circles.

'Sophia, be strong. For Antony,' Ioli said, rushing over to her.

'You don't believe any of this, do you?'

'I must admit, it has me puzzled.'

'God's glory is before you. You skeptics are always declaring that seeing is believing. Now, you are seeing and still...' Sophia paused for a second. 'You really want to help?'

'I'm here, aren't I?'

'Take my car. It's in the garage. Here are my keys. Drive

round the block and then come and park behind my house. I have to go to Saint Gerasimos church. Antony too, but if they see us leaving, they will follow.'

'Sure, right away,' Ioli said and took the keys. As she drove out of the garage, she saw the paramedic crew wheel out the poor girl from next door. The police fought to keep back the gang of reporters.

'Perfect timing, Ioli.' She smiled and turned down the street. She parked behind the house and soon Sophia and Antony appeared from behind the fence.

'Let's go and pray. I want to ask the Saint to spare Antony and give me the next wounds.'

'The next wounds?'

'If more stigmata follow, it will be the spear to the side.'

Ioli fastened her seatbelt, stepped on the gas and focused on the road, hoping her fingers would stop their sudden trembling. Antony buckled his safety belt and remained quiet during the short journey. Sophia, on the other hand, could not stop explaining to Ioli how Saint Gerasimos performed many miracles during his lifetime and even more after. She paused only to give Ioli the necessary directions. Soon, the car was turning left up a dirt road that led to a small, Byzantine, stone church. The old wooden door was shut and the place looked deserted.

'Is it open?' Ioli asked.

'Father Chrysostomo never locks.'

'Mother, I...'

'What's wrong sweetie?'

'I sense something. I think it is better we went home. We can pray to Saint Gerasimo there.'

'Don't be silly, my boy. It is a church. We are protected here. This is our home. Come on. Out,' Sophia ordered him with a peculiar smile. There was something off with the way Sophia spoke to him. A cold manner. She obviously cared for the lad; her words though, lacked real emotion.

The door creaked at every inch it was forced to take. The air inside was missing the freshness of the breeze outside. A scent of burning candles and oil lingered in the air. Sophia's three fingers met and the sign of the cross was formed three times. She made the sign again at every icon she approached and kissed, asking for God's blessing. Antony followed behind her, mimicking her every move. Ioli made her cross once and approached the central icon in the middle of the room. A large, heavy icon with two red, silk curtains, sat on a cherry wood easel.

'Ο ΑΓΙΟC ΓΕΡΑCΙΜΟC ΚΕΦΑΛΛΟΝΙΑC,' Ioli read the icon description. She gazed into the Saint's eyes, which seemed to follow you around the church. Sophia stood behind her, placing her arms gently on her shoulders.

'Ask him to spare Antony the pain.'

'I don't think I am the most suitable person...'

Sophia grabbed her hand and brought her down with her. The two women knelt before the Saint.

'In the name of the Father, the Son and the Holy Ghost, we ask you, Saint Gerasimo, blessed be your name, to spare your slave Antony from any further stigmata. Send them to me. Glorious may your name be. Glorious may be the mercy of God...'

Sophia continued with her praise as Ioli's head grew heavier and heavier by the minute. Her eyelids descended fast and she lost all control of her body. In a matter of seconds she collapsed into Sophia's lap.

Ioli awoke in a hazy environment or at least that is what her eyes were transmitting back to her brain. She squinted and tried to focus. Her head still felt heavy. An iron anchor inside her head, pulling her down. She jumped up in an effort to come back to full consciousness. Her feet did not follow her will. She felt two arms grab her and help her up. Her blurry vision got clearer by the minute. Sophia stood opposite her.

'Thank heavens you're well,' she said.

'What happened?' Ioli asked and felt the blood drip from her forehead.

'I guess Saint Gerasimo chose you instead,' Sophia replied calmly. Antony stood behind the golden framed icon, shaking in horror.

Ioli was lost for words. She wiped her face and looked down at her bloody hand. She took out her cell and turned her camera on. Soon, her screen was reflecting an image of an ashen Ioli with the same marks as Sophia's.

'He gave you the thorny crown and spared Antony. Thank you. Antony? Antony, speak up.'

'Thank you, Ioli. I told you, you were going to save me,' Antony said quietly with an awkward smile.

'Let's get you to the hospital...'

'No. No hospital. I am fine,' Ioli finally spoke. 'Just take me back to my hotel.'

Sophia looked upon her. She disapproved of her choice, yet did not argue. She nodded and complied with Ioli's wish.

Chapter Forty-Five

There is a certain magical aura floating in the air during summer nights in Greece. Especially on the islands. A feeling of living in a make-believe world. The heat of the day retreated with the sun, the sky dressed in sparkles, the moon came closer -or so it seemed- and shined brighter, the clean sea breeze lingered carelessly in the air and nature's sounds surrounded you.

Sophia sat in her porch's handmade rocking chair. Her late husband made it for her in celebration of their first summer in their then newly-bought house. She had tucked Antony in, cleaned the kitchen and now relaxed in the company of the good book. No evil television ever entered through her front door and never would.

She could read the Lord's word for hours. But tonight she found it difficult to focus.

'Vanity is a sin,' she told herself off as her mind travelled to tomorrow's long day. She was going to be interviewed by three different television programs. All from major networks. All ready to transmit her story across the country. Her chance to spread the word of Christ. She had already spoken to news reporters in the morning, but they only presented the story for a few seconds at the end of the news or planted the story on page eighteen of the daily paper. TV talk shows were the way to go.

'If only that silly cop would join me. Then, the story would be complete. We prayed to the Saint and he spared Antony, the poor, little, religious boy that felt God! And people always tend to disbelieve religious folk like me. But a woman like her, a police officer, they would have to believe...' she spoke out loud like it was the most normal thing to be talking loudly to yourself. She spoke in the same tone she would speak to a friend she invited over for evening coffee. Stress colored her last words. *They had to believe.*

Sophia placed her Bible carefully on a side table and stood up. She walked straight to the kitchen, opened the fridge door and took out a tiny bottle of Propofol. She opened the top drawer and searched clumsily for her box of needles. She injected the pointy end of the syringe into the see-through bottle, held them up and pulled down, filling it with the anesthetic drug. Needle in hand, she strolled to her bedroom, opened her bedside table's bottom drawer and pulled out her scarf with the carefully placed thorns inside.

She paused outside of Antony's room. She thought she would not have to put him through any more pain. Though, she had to be sure. Sure, that they all would believe. She turned the doorknob and entered his dimly lit room. The curtains flew up and down calmly, moved by the breeze sailing in through the open window. Saved on air conditioning for another month or so.

Antony slept peacefully. She tiptoed near him and

leaned over him. She injected him quickly, in the same way she had done before. He grunted and rolled to his side. She waited a few minutes for the drug to numb her boy and stood up, thorny scarf in hand.

'Step away from him, you bitch.'

Ioli's voice scared her from across the room. 'Your own son?' Ioli had leaped into the room through the open window, gun first and looked upon Sophia in disgust.

Sophia stood in shock. Frozen.

'Step back, now,' Ioli ordered.

A faint word escaped Sophia's pale lips. 'How...'

'I have a good sense of time lady. Besides, we entered that church with the sun low on the horizon and left with it nearly straight above us. You knocked me out for a good hour or so...'

'I did what I had to,' she whispered. 'Forgive me, I just wanted to spread the Lord's good word,' she apologized, taking a small step closer with every word.

'Stop right there.' Sophia paused, unsure of her next move.

'Your Lord told you to hurt your own flesh and blood? Your God is disgusted by you!'

Sophia let out a small scream and jumped at Ioli. Both women fell back onto the wall. Both with a good grip on the gun.

'You satanic whore. You will not stop the word from spreading,' Sophia screamed, pushing the gun towards Ioli's face. Ioli kicked Sophia hard in her stomach. Sophia bowed in pain, then bit hard into Ioli's flesh. Both fell to the ground, struggling for control of the gun.

Outside, Mrs. Callas ambled down her driveway, blue trash bag in hand. A loud bang made her jump. Her hand let go of the week's trash, while the other searched for her cell phone. As a can of coke rolled away and a smell of rotten chicken filled the air, the emergency operator answered.

'Kefalonia Police, what is your emergency?'

'I think I just heard a gunshot from my neighbor's house...'

Chapter Forty-Six

Yesterday's five hours of driving and four hours of interviewing relatives of the seven suicides, followed by two hours with the chief, were taking their toll. My back retaliated at every move, while my feet felt like ripping off my black derby shoes and spending the day soaking in the tub.

Piraeus port was in full swing. Cruise ships were flung out across the bay like God had just hit a gigantic piñata full of them. Buses arriving to pick up holiday makers from around the globe made traffic a living hell. Stuck there in limbo, I realized, I was going to be late for my final appointment with Ariadne. I could picture her judgmental eyes traveling to her wall clock, before coughing like a school teacher quietening down whispering pupils.

The evening sun reflected off the glass building, standing like a beacon calling out to me to make it on time. So near, yet so far. As I was contemplating abandoning my vehicle in the moving-an-inch-a-minute traffic, the line of cars came to life and started to roar. If I could only make it to the green light on time.

Orange. That will do just fine.

I swirled to the right and entered the building's underground parking lot. Sunlight gave way to neon lights as I headed down into the building's belly. In a hurry, I slid the car between a badly parked wagon and a graffiti-filled concrete wall.

'Hold the door,' I said, rushing up to the closing elevator doors. Three words I soon regretted. I spent the next few minutes listening to a whining eight year old who did not want to visit the dentist. The perfect soundtrack to my menacing migraine. I gladly exited on the 14th floor and felt sorry for the boy's mother. She had five more floors to go. I took a deep breath, pushed open the main door, smiled at the receptionist and rushed into Ariadne's office.

'Sorry for being late. Traffic is murder out there.'

'Nice choice of words,' she enigmatically said while gazing at her wall clock. 'I did not notice the time,' she lied.

'Analyzing me, already?' I fell back into the armchair, aware of my sweaty forehead and racing pulse. At least, my new deodorant acted as an ally against the hot weather. The cool room helped too.

Ariadne remained standing up behind her desk looking down at the morning paper.

'Never seen you read the paper before,' I commented.

'Catching up on the political scene. Don't own a TV,' she said without looking up.

'I hate politics. Isn't politics just money talking?'

'Hmm, I guess that's one way of looking at it.'

She walked over and sat opposite me, her beautiful legs crossed; her notepad on her lap.

'You failed the test.'

'What test?' I asked, causing her lips to form a smile.

'I wasn't reading anything in particular. I was being

silent. I wanted to see, if you could too, Costa.' She always pronounced my name in such a caring way.

'The quiet scares me because it speaks the truth...'

'And what is your truth?'

'I have had a hell of a year because of you.'

'Hell of a good time or hell of a bad time? You have had your ups and downs, your joys and worries.'

'Maybe you just gave me hell.'

Her emerald eyes crawled all over me. Searching, analyzing my body language, my facial expressions. She calmly collected her red hair off her shoulders and collected it up into a pony tail. Her high cheekbones, reddish from the sun.

'You are in a weird mood today.'

'Want to play along?'

'Meaning?'

'How about, today, I ask the questions for a change?'

'What kind of questions?'

'Personal ones.'

'Costa, that would be highly unprofessional of me. We are not at a cafe. This is my place of work. I...'

'I insist,' I said, pulling out my gun and placing it on my leg.

'Are you mad?' her cool undertone of a voice jumped up the decibel scale. However, it gave off the feeling of a well-rehearsed show. No emotion colored her words. No muscles twitched.

'Sit down, now!'

'Costa, what is this...'

'Shh,' I placed my finger on my lips. 'My turn to ask the questions. Remember?'

She raised both hands slowly and said, 'You're the man with the gun.'

'Were you born Maria Kontopoulou in Trikala, on the 4th of March 1975?'

'My past is my own. You have no right...'

'Maybe, I should have been more specific. Let's start with a few yes or no questions, before moving on to the whys. Were you born Maria Kontopoulou in Trikala, on the 4th of March 1975? *Yes* or *no*?'

She sat up straight. Her eyes, not flinching, gazed into mine. 'Yes.'

'Were you admitted to Trikala's CareForGirls institution at the age of thirteen, then run by the church? An institution for the mentally insane?'

'Well, that is not the proper term or...'

'Yes or no?' I stressed and picked up my gun.

'Yes.'

'You left the institution at eighteen, legally changed your name, left for Germany and came back a certified psychologist.'

'Do I answer to statements too? Yes. So you know my past. What are these shenanigans with the gun about?'

'Murder.'

'Murder? I haven't murdered anyone in my life.'

'From what I have seen, perhaps that sentence could even be true. Innocent, though, you are not. Your actions have murdered plenty.'

'Shall we stop beating around the bush, here? You come here to talk. Speak your mind freely. What is it you think I have done? What actions of mine have led to *murder*?' She mocked the last word.

'Giannis Keraunos.'

'Who?'

'Oh, come on, Ariadne. Don't play me for a fool. You are too intelligent to not remember a patient of yours.

1997, Katerini. You worked in the hospital's psychiatric ward.'

'Yes, I was a rising star back then. I worked miracles.'

'Giannis Keraunos,' I insisted.

'Mr. Keraunos was admitted into the ward by court order. After a string of violent incidents, he was finally arrested. When I met him, he was in an animal-like state, with clear signs of schizophrenia and had withdrawn from any type of human communication. Doctors had pretty much given up on him...'

'Until, you came along.'

'Until, I came along and got through to him.'

'Got through to him, alright.'

'Yes, I did. Three years later he was released on good behavior.'

'After, *you* deemed him healthy.'

'He was.'

'Yes, because everybody in their right mind, joins a monastery, becomes an abbot, brainwashes the monks into believing he has a holy book and sets them on a course of death.'

'That is not my fault. Religion got to him. That happened after me.'

'Really? So you deny meeting him again?'

Her head tilted to the right. She studied me.

'There is nothing you can charge me with.' Her eyes crawled around my chest.

I smiled. 'You believe that I am wired?'

She signed a I-don't-know with her hands. She was a lady that took no chances.

'I would even bet, you gave him the *holy* book.'

She did not reply.

'After all, you do have a thing about religion, right?'

'Are we back to the yes or no game again?'

'I bet you loved treating Father Avgoustino during your holidays in Santorini. Got a nice little vacation house on the outskirts of town, near his church, haven't you?'

'Yes, I own property there. Is that a crime? Yes, pro bono, I agreed to have sessions with the priest. He came to me. Is that a crime too?' She acted as if she was getting bored with me.

'You twisted his mind. A priest quoting Freud and teaching Kate what a Cinderella Syndrome was. I bet you saw him frequently. I bet you played your evil mind tricks on him...'

'You make me sound like a witch. I talked with the old man. His religion was oppressing him. He needed a release. All I did was to advise him to deal with all the sins he could not bear to hear anymore. By all means, I did not intend for him to set his sinners on each other.'

I sat there, quietly, staring at her.

'What?' she asked, annoyed by my silence.

'I can picture you in court. All dressed up, playing your act.'

'And the jury declaring me not guilty.'

'You have it all planned out, haven't you? Was your family that bad? What the hell happened to you in that institution?'

'Yes. You have no idea. Hell. There, I answered all three of your questions.'

'No remorse? None, whatsoever?'

'Remorse? A word for the weak.'

'Not even for the seven people you convinced to take their own lives?' I started to lose my cool.

She looked around, uncomfortable with the tension. Her fingers ran along her legs, just before her arms crossed.

'I underestimated you. You *are* good, Captain. I'll give you that.'

'Is that all you have to say?'

'What do you want me to say? There are too many buttons in this world. So what if I pushed a few? Weaklings, the lot of them. Coming in here, crying about this and that. They were practically begging for someone to offer them a way out. Life was too much for them to handle.'

'Oh, cut the crap, Ariadne. So righteous, aren't you? Is that what your sick mind tells you? Why these seven? Huh? Tell me that!'

'As I said, weaklings...'

'Bullshit! You love your sick, manipulating games. They were all religious. You loved that. And you chose them because of their names. Random killings, just like a heartless sociopath with a gun.'

Her jaw dropped slightly. I was yelling; my face colored red by anger. I waved the gun up and down. I stood up, taking small steps towards her. With every step, I yelled a name.

'**A**gatha. **R**ita. **I**dalia. **A**nastasia. **D**emetris. **N**ikolas. **E**ftichia. A-R-I-A-D-N-E. Ariadne!' With the sound of her name, I raised the gun to her eye level.

'Going to shoot me, Costa?'

'I should. Would be doing this world a favor.'

Her hands jumped and grabbed the end of my pistol. She placed her forehead at the end of the barrel.

'Kill me then. I've been dead inside since I was born.'

'Ariadne Metaxa, you are under arrest for conspiracy to murder...'

'I promised myself, I'd never be locked up again. And think of this, mighty Captain. How many out there have I triggered? How many are out there as we speak, are ready to do the unthinkable? You cannot even begin to comprehend my elaborate plans; how deep my network goes. You dare arrest me and you will never be safe. Tracy will never be safe. I have patients ready to rape and kill at my *suggestion*.' An evil smile decorated her face. Her green eyes glowing with passion.

'Don't you dare threaten Tracy...'

'Or what? Come on, macho man. Shoot me, shoot me!' she yelled, standing up.

'Turn around and place your hands behind your back. Now!'

She turned slowly. My handcuffs and I approached her arms. Ariadne let out a small wild scream and ran straight for the glass wall, throwing herself at it. The glass shattered and out Ariadne went. I ran and looked down. She fell with a smile. She fell taking her demons with her. Her pale skin became one with the hot, grey pavement below. Her blood oozed out, filling in the gaps left by her brains and parts of skin tissue.

Chapter Forty-Seven

MARIA'S (ARIADNE'S) STORY

Trikala, 1975

'My water just broke,' Irene shouted over the sports announcer who was screaming ecstatically from the TV set. She stood in the doorway, hand on belly, with a puddle forming between her bare feet.

'Can it wait ten minutes? The game is almost over and...'

'No, Andrea, it can't fucking wait. You serious? Get your fat ass up and take me to the hospital. Now!'

'You're lucky you're pregnant or I...'

'Yeah, yeah. You're the man. Now, let's go get this kid of yours out.'

He reluctantly forced himself up from the ripped brown couch, switched off the television and looked around for his pants. He pulled up his old jeans, scratched his balls, lit a cigarette and headed for the car, leaving his wife to carry her bag.

'What about the kids?' he asked as the car's engine came to life.

'I locked all three of them in Gianni's bedroom with a bunch of toys. My sister will come by later. I left them food and water,' she said casually. It was not the first time the kids were left unattended.

A few hours and a bunch of curse words later, their fourth child and first girl came into the world.

Little Maria was sickly pale with a patch of ginger hair stuck on top of her head. Her eyes a rather dull shade of grey.

'Little ugly, isn't she?'

'Oh, shut up, Andrea.'

That was the first of a long line of insults, Maria would hear during her life with them.

Both her parents kept busy with their farm all day and spent most of the night watching trash TV and drinking a combination of cheap beers and homemade wine. Her three older brothers never paid much attention to her either. Used to their own violent games, they needed no girl to disturb them with *girlie* things.

Maria did not utter a single word until the age of two and she did not walk properly until the age of three, having no one to encourage or support her for either important task.

She quickly regretted learning how to walk. It signaled the start of slavery for the little girl. As she got older, her parents forced to sweep, dust, mop, help with the cooking, scrub the toilets and do the laundry. All the boys had to do was help out with the animals. They got to play and watch television for the rest of the day, while Maria carried out her chores until the owls awoke and hooted, much to Andreas' annoyance. He often threatened to shoot them, but as with most of his talk, it remained just that.

The only times Maria relaxed were on Sunday mornings when the family played *pretend*. They all wore their best outfits and headed over to their local church. It was the only time, her mother combed her hair. It was the only time, mother smiled at her. She knew it was fake and for others to see, but it still warmed her little heart. Yes, Sundays were the best. She even got to bathe Saturday night and enjoy the feeling of waking up shiny and new. Father still did not pay any attention to her, but even that came as great news. It was far better than being ordered to do this and that all day, being smacked with every excuse and listening to his whining about how girls were worthless and hard to get rid of.

'Where are we going to find money to marry off a girl?' he whined as he drank his fifth beer.

At age nine, Maria decided to ask her parents if she could stay on after church and attend katixitiko, the Sunday school run by the priest.

'No way in hell,' her father grunted. 'Who will help your mother with Sunday dinner? Clean up afterwards? Sunday is a man's rest day, if you aren't here, your mother will have to do everything on her own. Are you that spoiled and ungrateful? You will never find a husband with that attitude!'

'It finishes by half eleven, daddy.' She hated using that word, but she needed to sweeten him up. 'I promise, I'll run straight home and help out. Please, daddy, please.'

He paused and took on his thinking pose. She had started to win him over.

'Oh, Andrea, let her go,' her mother stuck up for her. A

rare occasion. 'It's church. And besides, today, Maria's teacher told me that she is excellent in class. Her best pupil!'

Andrea groaned something about women not needing a brain, before reluctantly agreeing she went to katixitiko. In the heat of the moment, Maria leaped forward and for the first time in her life, she hugged her father. Andrea was caught off guard and patted her on the head, calling her a good girl.

'She isn't a dog, Andrea,' his wife laughed.

Next Sunday and every Sunday after that, Maria eagerly awaited for the liturgy to be over and Sunday school to start. Her brothers picked on her and called her a number of names ranging from 'religious nerd' to 'Virgin Mary, the ugly version'.

Maria did not care.

She cherished the moments she sat in a circle with another fifteen kids and listened to Father Anastasios retell stories from the Bible and from the life of Greek Saints.

She glowed with joy, knowing that there was someone in her life that truly loved her, and that was Jesus. He became the one she turned to, late at night, when after a tiring day of chores and put downs, she needed a release. Someone to talk to.

She loved Father Anastasios for introducing her to a new world of endless love and kindness. Used to cleaning up, she would stay for another ten minutes, after school was out, and tidy up the small room beside the elderly man's chambers. She tidied their books neatly back on their shelves, pushed chairs back into position and washed the plastic cups left by the children in the dirty sink. She wished she had more time to stay on. The whole place begged for a good scrub. Father Anastasios was left a widower, many years back and as a man from a different era, he did not maintain his humble home well.

One rainy spring day, the kind with bright rainbows, Maria was busy washing up the same plastic cups she had washed so many times before, over the last two years. She stood by the sink, enjoying the view outside. Maria had turned into a fine, young lady. Beautiful porcelain skin, red, straight hair and emerald eyes full of life.

'Anything else I can do, Father?'

'Oh, my dear. You have done plenty. Now it's my turn to repay you,' he smiled.

It had become Maria's favorite part of the day. She rushed and picked up a brand new picture Bible from the top shelf and passed it on to Father Anastasios, who was sitting in his large, green armchair. She sat on his lap and placed her head on his chest.

'David and Goliath,' he said, giving weight to his voice. Maria gazed at the picture of the skinny youth with the slingshot, standing so brave opposite the enormous, menacing giant.

Father Anastasios was a great storyteller. A natural, with a voice that would be envied by the most experienced CNN news reporters. She had sat on his lap countless times before and listened to how Adam and Eve lost paradise, Moses parted the sea, Abraham nearly killed his son, Samson lost his hair, and of course, about her hero, Jesus.

This time, they held the book together. Father with his left hand and Maria with her right.

'… Then David rushed forth, slingshot in hand…' Father Anastasios read, while placing his right hand upon Maria's leg. She thought nothing of it, at first. She even curled up more into his arms.

She did not feel as comfortable, when his hand travelled

slightly up her thigh. Neither did she feel comfortable, when at the end of the story, Father Anastasios's hand brushed against her breast as she stood up.

'Have a nice day, child,' he said as if nothing had happened.

Maria ran home that day.

Reaching the gate to her home, she wiped her tears and shook off her confused state. She had chores to do.

Late at night, she lay in her bed wondering if she had mistaken Father Anastasios's intentions. He was rather old and he did love her like a daughter. She must have misjudged him. She could not accept that Father Anastasios, *her* Father Anastasios was one of *those* men.

Next Sunday took its time to arrive.

Her anticipation prolonged its arrival. Preoccupied with her thoughts, she sat through mass and Sunday school staring at the clock. Half past eleven. Finally, everyone left and she was alone with him. She tidied up in a rush and quickly picked up the colorful children's Bible. She hopped on his lap and opened the book. She held the book with both her hands, leaving his hands free. She needed to test her theory. She needed to prove he was her saintly guardian.

As Noah finished the ark, she felt his hands on her thighs. She wore a blue dress, knee high. Soon, his hand had managed to find its way under her skirt. A tear fell from her eye as she felt his dirty fingers journey up her leg. Just before reaching his intended destination, Maria screamed at the top of her lungs. It was a wild, animal-like scream.

'How dare you? You filthy, old man,' she yelled, jumping up. She swung the Bible hard round and hit him on the head.

'My child, you misunderstood…'

'Fuck you!' she screamed the words she had heard many times before by her parents and ran out the door.

She ran faster than ever before. The mountain land-scape around her fading into a blur as the wind blew directly at her, wiping her continuous flow of tears. She did not stop running until she reached her garden's green gate. She had to gather herself. Unsure what to say, unsure how and what to explain, she decided to pause her ordeal. With maturity beyond her years, she acted as if nothing had happened and went on with helping her mother with Sunday dinner. Chicken and potatoes again.

Bedtime came quickly and soon she was alone, able to think. She felt disgusted by Father Anastasios's actions. She always hated the way her father groped her mother. Love seemed very cheap to her. She curled up, pushing back her filthy sheets. She could still feel his hands on her.

Suddenly, her door flew open. Her dad stormed into her room, anger flashing in his eyes. He was huffing and puff-ing; his hands clenched into a punch. Her mother stood behind him. Her worried look caused shivers down Maria's spine.

'You little whore. You little bitch...' The words colored with hate, coming out one by one with heavy breathing.

'Dad, what...'

'Don't you play innocent with me!' he yelled. 'There I was, with my mates at the coffee shop and I get pulled aside by Father Anastasios...' Her eyes opened wide, her jaw in free fall. '... And he tells me that you stay after Sunday school and ask him to read stories for you and you ask to sit on his lap and rub yourself against him...'

'That's a lie!'

'Shut it,' he screamed.

'No,' she yelled back. 'He touched me. I did nothing.' Her mother started to sob.

'You disgusting, little slut. You have shamed this family...' He did not continue his sentence. He just unloosened his black leather belt and approached her slowly.

The first strike hurt the worst. The belt slapped against her white, tender skin, cutting into it.

The shock of being beaten like one of his farm animals, as if a stubborn donkey refusing to move, blocked out the pain of the next eight strikes. Her skinny arms tried to cover her face, only causing more anger to her father. He lifted her up by the hair and threw her bleeding body to the hard, cold floor.

'Mama, please help...' she started to say, only to be kicked hard in the mouth. Blood shot out and her mother screamed.

'Andrea, you are killing her.'

Andrea knelt on top of Maria and whispered evilly into her ear.

'You are grounded for life. No school, no church, no friends, nothing.'

The next morning, Maria awoke, bruised and sore on the floor. She had passed out and her parents had left her there. It was her first day as an animal. She did not feel human anymore. She did not get treated like one anymore. Both her parents looked upon her in utter disgust. They barked orders at her and took joy *removing the demon from inside her* as they said, by having her scrub the entire house with a bar of soap and an old toothbrush. They both took turns in beating her at night. She was not allowed to talk, look them in the eyes, shower or eat with the family. She served them all dinner and stood silently in the corner. When the family had finished, only then was she allowed to eat their leftovers. Her brothers quickly picked up on what was going on and joined the family *fun*. They pushed her around and called her names and ordered her around. Once, she tried to ask her older brother for help, only to receive his spit on her face, followed by the line 'Do not speak to me, whore.'

She hated them for everything. She hated Father Anastasios. She hated her life.

The fatal night arrived on a sweet summer day.

She lay in bed, bones aching from a tiring day. Her eyelids journeyed down and began to cover her eyes. That was when she heard her window open. She sat up and watched in terror as a stranger entered and stood in her room. She opened her mouth, ready to scream but the young man leaped upon her. His hand covered her mouth. She recognized him now. He was their neighbor's sixteen year old son.

'Shh, don't move or I will hurt you,' he whispered uneasily. More of a pep talk for his ears than a threat. 'I paid your brother for a good time.' His free hand fell upon her breast. Maria bit down hard and did not let go. She felt his blood drip into her mouth. He pulled back in pain, leaving skin behind.

'Get out!'

'Now, listen here, whore. I paid good money...'

He did not finish his sentence. The doorknob rattled and the youth ran to the window. Her father entered the room, just in time to see the lad flee the scene.

'You dirty little cunt. You dare bring men under my roof?'

She had no time to react, to explain. He grabbed her by the hair and dragged her out of the house and into the barn. The rough and rocky ground cut into her body, and animal manure stuck to her body and hair. Andrea picked her up, slapped her around and kicked her back down to the dirt. He fell on top of her, ripping off her clothes. He, then, stood up and lifted her up by her hair, ignoring her screams. He walked over to the pigsty and, without a second thought, he threw her in the mud.

'Welcome to your new home,' he said, spat on the floor and left.

Maria stood up, covered in mud. The pigs began to surround her. She jumped out of the muddy environment and sat down in the pile of hay. She promised not to cry. She sat there still, for over an hour, thoughts running freely inside her mind's darkest corners. This had to end.

The red gasoline tank was heavy, but her anger provided her with extra strength. The house opposite her stood silent, everyone was asleep. She strolled around the house wearing only mud, pig feces and an evil, twisted smile. Gasoline leaked out as she went. She walked up the porch steps, leaving fuel puddles behind. A snake-like line of gasoline followed her into the kitchen. She quietly opened the top drawer and took out a pack of matches. She emptied the ten-liter tank outside her parent's door, said her goodbyes and exited the house. She took the tank back to its place in the barn, took a deep breath and went back to the house. She stood outside and lit a match. She used it to light the whole box and dropped the box on the wooden porch steps.

Blue flames rose alive and red fire ran around the house. Maria took a few steps back and sat down in the dirt, the flames reflecting in her hollow eyes. The corners of her smile moved upwards at the sound of the first screams. Thick, black smoke climbed out of open windows and gaps in the roof. A loud bang came as the fire reaching the kitchen and the small, wooden house collapsed, burying all her problems.

Maria did not move a muscle. Not even when the fire truck arrived. Not even when the tall policeman tried to get answers from her. Not even when the paramedics picked her up. She did not even speak or show any kind of emotion when two days later she was informed that none of her family had survived.

'Who started the fire, Maria? We know it was no accident,' the police questioned her over and over again. Maria did not utter a word. Her silence puzzled investigators. They could not blame her for anything. They did not have any proof of any wrong-doing on her behalf. They washed their hands of the case and passed it over to the hospital's psych ward.

The hospital's psychiatrist and the local judge decided on sending her to CareForGirls. An institution set up by nuns for troubled, underage girls. She was to remain there until the age of eighteen and to be treated for shock and grief.

At the institution, Maria lost the only thing left to her. Her faith.

The institution was a fine example of a shiny shop window with all its goods on display. On paper, it was a great project. In reality, it was a prison for girls who got into trouble and society needed somewhere to get rid of them. The nuns thought of the girls as sinners and as such, needed to be punished. Thieves, whores, drug addicts all under the same roof. All made to work long hours for free at the monastery's laundry service and bakery. The nuns received the money and the girls received a piece of bread, luke-warm soup and a good beating.

God was nowhere to be found.

Maria realized He did not exist. He was just a story, a fable made up for people like her parents to look good on

Sundays, for people like Father Anastasios to place his dirty paws on young girls and for 'wicked bitches' like the nuns to use His name to get rich and to abuse weaklings that had nowhere to go, no-one to turn to.

Intelligent as she was, she enjoyed listening to the psychiatrist who came from the hospital twice a week and had sessions with most of the girls. His job fascinated her. The way he tried to dig up memories, to get her to *open up*. To *force* her to see things *his* way.

What gave her more joy though, was manipulating her fellow inmates. She loved how easy it was to get them to do something, to start a fight, to wind them up and watch them go.

Years went by and her eighteenth birthday came. She woke up a free woman. With her head up high, she marched out the gates. A woman with a plan. A deadly plan.

Twenty one years and dozens of bodies later, her flesh became one with the ground.

'May her soul rest in peace,' a worker at the crematorium whispered as he lit the fire.

A kind police captain waited outside to receive her ashes.

Chapter Forty-Eight

I rushed out of the room, running past Ariadne's assistant who stood frozen in shock by the door. The thunderous clinking sound of glass breaking called her into the room. I maniacally pushed the elevator call button; my knees shaking in anticipation. As the doors opened and I jumped in, her assistant gathered enough strength to take a few steady steps towards the broken window. She looked down below and fell back. Her blood froze and her hand covered her mouth, silencing short, uncontrollable screams.

The patrol car awaiting my exit with a handcuffed Ariadne, had already called the incident in and both officers stood feet away from the twisted body, prepared to hold nosy people back.

Back and feet aching, sweating from all corners and with my heart beat racing fast enough to win the Kentucky Derby, I ran out onto the street. I paused at the sight of Ariadne's body. In all my years of being called to examine body after body, I had never seen a jumper before. After being in free fall from the 14th floor, her body slammed into the solid concrete ground below. It did not look human anymore; it had lost its shape. Bones gave in and skin tissue spread across the grey pavement. Her arms and legs, bent in an unnatural way, emerged out of a large pool of dark red blood and gore.

The howling sound of the speeding ambulance's siren startled me. The paramedics jumped out of the vehicle, only to realize their difficult task ahead. To gather all pieces of the body. I stepped back and fell down onto a metal bench, warm from hours under the Mediterranean sun. I ducked my head, not able to watch. Unlike the crowd that had gathered behind the yellow tape with their gadgets held high, hoping to get a glimpse of something gruesome to show their friends. Soon, the vultures of the media would arrive.

Society is in free fall too, circling around, heading down the toilet drain. Too much shit...

'Costa?' the familiar sweet concerned voice came from the figure towering over me.

'I had just walked into the station, when the boys called it in,' Ioli said. She sat down beside me, her right arm stroking my back.

'Are you okay? You seem...'

'I'm fine. Just taking a moment to scold myself for everything I could have done differently. I shouldn't have confronted her. I should...'

'You aren't responsible for her actions. This was her choice.'

'A choice she felt was the only one I had left her with.'

'Then she got her wish. This was what she wanted. She chose this, rather than prison.'

We sat in silence for a while, in total contrast to the mayhem around us. Police and paramedics were coming and going, the forensics team opened kits and collected evidence, reporters shouted questions at every direction and of course, cell phones danced around in the air.

'By the way, where the heck have you been?' I asked.

She chuckled. 'I wish I knew where to begin. It all started with a boy with stigmata and ended with me shooting his mother. She's critical but stable.'

I stared at her for a split second. I exhaled deeply and bit my lower lip. I let it play around, grinding against my teeth.

'Just another day on the clock, right?' I finally spoke.

'Just another day.'

Epilogue

The promontory of Sounio overlooks the wild waters of the Aegean and is home to the ruins of Poseidon's temple, perched on the headland. The remains of the once grand place of worship are a sought-after site, offering majestic sunsets. A clear view of the great Greek sun dipping into the ocean, coloring the waves multiple shades of orange.

The ships below danced up and down upon the waves. Tour buses were unloading groups of tourists while the parking was full from Athenians on day excursions.

Ioli and I ignored the dirt road leading up to the temple and preferred to hike down the peninsula. We reached mighty rocks, standing strong against the sea and fierce wind currents. I climbed on top of the tallest one and pulled Ioli up. She was holding the brass urn, given to me at the crematorium. Ariadne had no known next of kin. In her will, she donated everything to University of Athens and requested to be cremated.

The sun was moments away from vanishing into the sea.

'Am I supposed to say something?'

Ioli raised her shoulders. 'Beats me.'

'God, if you can hear me, please provide Ariadne with the peace she lacked in life.'

'And please, can you do a better job at being God? Things are going to hell down here,' Ioli added and then, crossed herself out of fear of blasphemy.

I took off the urn's lid and held it up high in the air. As I tilted it, ashes flew out into the wind and quickly scattered. The charcoal cloud vanished from in front of us.

'A whole person, gone in a second...' I whispered.

We sat down upon a huge stone near the edge, enjoying the scenery and the sound of the waves crashing into the rocks.

'Don't lose your faith, Cara,' I said.

'It's not so much about losing my faith. It's a feeling of disappointment. Disappointment in God, society, church... the whole system. Life should be so much more than this.'

'Maybe this is all just a test or at least that is what my grandma used to call life.'

'Well, it feels like a fucking tricky algebra test. It could at least be a multiple choice test.'

'You're a weird one, Cara.'

'That's rich coming from you.'

We both laughed out loud and it felt revitalizing.

Soon, seagulls squawked around us, as the birds came to land for the night.

'We better be heading back up before total darkness,' Ioli said.

It got darker by the minute and if it were not for the temple's bright spotlights, I believe we would still be wandering around.

The next day, life continued as it always does. A

morning kiss, the day's first rich aromatic coffee, the uphill journey to work, the smile of co-workers, my office chair.

Ioli sat buried in paperwork concerning her stigmata case. I, too, had tons of forms to fill in.

The loud discordant sound of an incoming call lifted our heads out of our papers.

A new day, a new case.

vinci-books.com/DeathOfABride

A bride. A murder. An island with nowhere to hide.

When a bride is found murdered on her wedding day, a storm
traps every guest on the remote island of Gadvos. Captain
Papacosta and Lieutenant Cara must unmask the killer before they
strike again—because everyone's a suspect, and no one is safe.

Turn the page for a free preview…

Death of a Bride: Chapter One

Of all the plans a bride makes for her wedding day, dying is definitely not one of them.

Cassandra Zampetaki crept out of her family's mansion and dashed through the pouring rain, past the thrashing swimming pool and into the safety of the stone brick pool house. She quickly closed the glass door behind her, gasping to catch her breath. Blustery winds roamed the hilltop and fat drops of water crashed down mightily from the night sky. Nothing outside could compare with the storm inside Cassandra. Tomorrow she would walk down the aisle and become Mrs. Cassandra Cara-Zampetaki. Her mother had insisted she keep her last name.

'It's a name with history behind it. What is a 'Cara'? A barbarian name...'

'Mother!' Cassandra would interrupt her and shoot a disapproving stare towards her.

Cassandra pulled the thick vermilion curtains shut and turned on the lights. The expensive handcrafted chandelier came to life and pushed shadows back into corners.

Cassandra ran her hands through her long, copper hair. She squeezed out as much water as she could and let the drops fall to the cold floor. She tied her hair up in a bun and stripped down to her underwear. Her fingers played with her gold engagement ring. It had been in Homer's family for five generations and she felt proud to have it gracing her hand.

With her heartbeat thrumming, she opened the doors of the heavy, wooden wardrobe and with a slight smile, she gazed at her wedding dress. She did not know why she felt compelled, but she had to try it on, just one more time before the *big day*. She struggled to wear it on her own but soon, the silk, white Valentino dress settled on her curvy figure. She tiptoed to the wall mirror and twirled in delight.

As she spun, her eye caught a glimpse of a shadowed figure sitting behind her in the corner of the room. Her hand instinctively covered her faint scream as she tripped and fell to the tiled floor. The shadowy figure rolled her wheelchair into the light.

'Oh, it's you,' Cassandra said and exhaled deeply, obvious relief spreading across her diamond-shape face. 'You gave me such a fright. What are you doing here?' Her voice climbed the decibel scale, going from abject nervousness to slight anger.

'I came here in the evening to enjoy the sunset over the cliffs and when the storm grew stronger and stronger, I decided to stay here,' the old lady said.

'Oh, Mrs. Lakioti, why didn't you call up to the house?' Cassandra thought of the evening feast the woman had missed out on. No one had noticed her missing. She had been alone for hours.

'Now that is what I call a wedding dress. You look like an angel, my dear.'

'Thank you.' Cassandra turned back around and stared into the mirror. 'It was love at first sight. I knew this was *the* dress from the moment the saleslady carried it out. Of course, mother found it too plain...' Cassandra chattered away. Her flow of words covered the sound of stealthy footsteps behind her. The knife came down hard and sliced into her back. The acute, agonizing pain brought Cassandra to her knees. Before shock settled, the blade was yanked out of her fake-tanned skin. Cassandra screamed, only to be silenced by a second stabbing; this time straight into her throat. Blood sprayed onto the mirror and ran down the white dress, coloring it crimson red on its way down. The bride fell forward, eyes wide open, hands desperately seeking something to grasp. Outside, the storm grew even more violent; constant thunder broke through the air and howling, gale force winds uprooted old trees, while rain pummelled the grooved roof. Inside, Cassandra's last breath departed from her trembling lips and her body glided down the glass surface.

Her killer stepped into the pool of blood forming under her wedding dress. Garden cutters approached Cassandra's ring finger and with force, her murderer cut through the bone.

Death of a Bride: Chapter Two

Three weeks ago

'Costa, get up! And turn that hell-sent alarm clock off,' my lovely-*after*-her-morning-coffee wife moaned.

My eyes struggled to open and my hand clumsily searched for my alarm ringing cell phone amongst my pile of sci-fi books. *I really need to switch to Kindle, soon.* I slammed my hand down, offering silence to our warm bedroom.

'Shit, I'm late,' I said, realizing the time.

'Yes, I know. It's the third time that damn thing has woken me up. You kept on pressing snooze.'

I jumped out of bed and rushed into the bathroom. 'Going to get up and have breakfast?' I shouted to Tracy as I scratched my aching back and peed out last night's Tennessee whiskey.

'No way! It's my day off and I'm planning on going back to sleep. Now, stop talking to me and close the door.'

'Lucky you,' I replied, got dressed in a hurry, laid a kiss upon her warm cheek and sprinted out the door.

Root canal procedure. Stepping on Lego bricks while barefoot. Morning traffic in Athens. All inevitable evils of life.

I rolled down my Audi's front passenger windows and enjoyed the slight, November breeze. I accepted the fact that I was going to be late for work and relaxed amid in the chaos of honks and curse words that polluted the air. Thirty-five minutes later, I had parked in the underground parking of police headquarters. The air that hung between the grey, concrete walls was stale and thick with cigarette smoke lingering amongst it. Ever since administration banned smoking inside the police cafeteria, the parking and the roof became everyone's new hot spot.

I waved good morning to other officers on their way out for the morning's second coffee and third cigarette -all while their card had been punched in, of course.

The newly installed elevator carried me up to the fifth floor. I opened my brown briefcase and took out a few solved case files. I walked down the long corridor -that passed by fellow homicide Lieutenants' and Captains' offices- acting busy, ducked down into my papers, pretending to be reading them.

I am not late, I am busy.

I finally reached my office's glass door, grabbed the cool handle with my sweaty palm and with relief of not bumping into the grumpy, I-hate-people-being-late chief, I entered the two-desk room. Cherry scented air welcomed me. Ioli had already lit her candles. She disliked the smell of confined, office air.

Ioli looked up from her computer screen and grinned.

'Well, look at the party animal coming in late.'

'Shut up.'

'Good morning to you too, boss.'

'You look... fresh. I mean after all those drinks I saw you gulp down.'

She flashed her trademark smile. 'First of all, I did not realize you were going to chaperone me at your wife's birthday party. Second, I am a Cretan. We never get drunk. Third, most drinks were just orange juice. It's a defence mechanism. Keeps me busy, instead of looking like a Parthenon pillar. I can't dance to save my life. You on the other hand, burned the dance floor after consuming a month's supply of Jack.'

I rubbed my forehead. 'Don't remind me.'

'Midlife crisis getting worse?'

'Screw you!' I threw my head back and laughed. 'I was just happy to see Tracy having fun. And having friends! She doesn't say it or show it, but it hasn't been easy moving to Greece from New York. Actually, it was really the first time we both had fun since Gaby's death.'

Ioli's face darkened. 'I can't imagine how it must feel to lose a child...'

'There's no getting used to it or moving on or accepting it as part of life. You just keep living with a part of you missing.'

Awkward silence filled the room. Ioli was not only my partner; she was my best friend. However, too much honesty is not always a good thing. It was too early in the morning for such a depressing, *downer* conversation.

'What time did you leave the party?' I asked, redirecting the conversation back to the previous night.

'Around midnight. Cinderella had to get back to her parents.'

'I forgot that they are visiting. How's that working out?'

'Horrible. I love my parents, but they've been here three days now and I am suffocating. Mama keeps cooking and cleaning, and Papa keeps asking me when am I planning on getting married and offering him grandchildren. He keeps saying his heart won't last too long and going on about how the doctors said he should take it easy and enjoy his golden years with family. Hell, I tell you, hell. They want to see you, by the way. Their daughter's savior.'

'I wouldn't call me that...'

'Well, they do. They even want to invite you to my cousin's wedding next month. Both you and Tracy. My whole family is dying to meet you.'

'Wedding? We don't even know the bride or groom...'

Ioli burst out laughing. 'In so many ways, you are still so freakin' American. Half the people at Greek weddings don't know the couple. Parents and the family invite most of the guests. Anyway, mama said it would be a nice vacation for us all and it's her way of re-paying you, Greek-style. She will house you and feed you. I'm the one who is going to have the hardest time, listening to how my aunts are all marrying off their younger-than-me offspring and Giannis's and Anna's thirty-five year old, only child is a homicide cop living alone in Athens.'

'Is the wedding in Chania?'

'No. In Gavdos.'

'Where? Is that a small Cretan village, I have never heard of?'

'It's an island actually. Only geography nerds and nudist know its existence.'

'You are a weird one, Cara. Why would only geography nerds and nudist know its existence?'

'Here, let me show you.' She swung round her computer screen and typed in Gavdos. Images of a small, triangular dot below Crete appeared in the first row of pictures. A caption read: THE MOST SOUTHERN POINT OF

EUROPE. Deserted beaches with the sign NUDIST PARADISE, followed.

'Please tell me, it's not a nude wedding.'

'Stop making me laugh. Of course not, it's winter next month and freezing cold winds roam the island. Men would never agree to it.' Her laughter made it difficult to hear all her words clearly. 'The bride is from there. The wedding will take place at her mother's mansion. Her family is the richest family on the island, out of all sixty inhabitants.'

'That few?'

'Probably fewer in the winter. Until recently, the island did not even have electricity. Everything worked with generators.'

'Sounds lovely.' I raise my thick eyebrows and looked away.

'Don't be sarcastic. We'll have a great time. I don't want to go alone anyway.'

'Need a chaperone again?'

'I need a boyfriend to be honest. Someone to show off to my evil cousins and aunts and then dump the next day.' She fixed her high ponytail and turned back to her computer.

'Why dump him?' I dared to ask.

'Last thing on my mind...'

'So you say, so you say...'

I fell back, into my white, leather desk chair and stared at the phone. I needed a good case to wake me up.

Grab your copy...
vinci-books.com/DeathOfABride

About the Author

Luke Christodoulou is an Amazon bestselling author, a poet and an English teacher (MA Applied Linguistics - University of Birmingham). He is, also, a coffee-movie-book-Nutella lover.

His first book, THE OLYMPUS KILLER (#1 Bestseller - Thrillers), was released in April, 2014. The book was voted Book Of The Month for May on Goodreads (Psychological Thrillers). The book continued to be a fan favorite on Goodreads and was voted BOTM for June in the group Nothing Better Than Reading. In October, it was BOTM in the group Ebook Miner, proving it was one of the most talked-about thrillers of 2014.

The second stand-alone thriller from the series, THE CHURCH MURDERS, was released April, 2015 to widespread critical and fan acclaim. The Church Murders became a bestseller in its categories throughout the summer and was nominated as Book Of The Month in three different Goodreads groups.

DEATH OF A BRIDE was the third Greek Island Mystery to be released. Released in April, 2016 it followed in the footsteps of its successful predecessors. From its first week in release it hit the number one spot for books set in Greece.

MURDER ON DISPLAY came out in 2017 and enriched the series.

HOTEL MURDER, the fifth and 'final' book in the series, followed in early 2018.

In 2018, his box set of mysteries became an international bestseller.

Luke Christodoulou has also ventured into 'children's book land' and released 24 MODERNIZED AESOP FABLES, retelling old stories with new elements and settings. The book, also, features sections for parents, which include discussions, questions, games and activities.

In 2019, TWELVE MONTHS OF MURDER came out, his first collection of shorts.

His first novel outside of the Greek Island Mysteries collection came in 2020, maintaining his love for a Greek theme. A supernatural thrill ride with the name of BEWARE OF GREEKS BEARING GIFTS.

PANDORA'S BOX followed in 2021. A mind-twisting whodunit set in his favorite Greek town, the seaside resort of Parga. The following year saw the release of the highly anticipated ACHILLES' HEEL.

His first YA murder mystery, SENIOR YEAR MURDERS was released in 2024, hitting the charts for young adult thrillers.

He is currently working on various projects (which he is secretive about).

He resides in Limassol, Cyprus with his loving wife, his chatty daughter and his super-energetic son.

Hobbies include travelling the Greek Islands discovering new food and possible murder sites for his stories. He, also, enjoys telling people that he 'kills people for a living'.